ULTRA

DAVID CARROLL

Scholastic Canada Ltd.
Toronto New York London Auckland Sydney
Mexico City New Delhi Hong Kong Buenos Aires

Scholastic Canada Ltd.
604 King Street West, Toronto, Ontario M5V 1E1, Canada

Scholastic Inc.
557 Broadway, New York, NY 10012, USA

Scholastic Australia Pty Limited
PO Box 579, Gosford, NSW 2250, Australia

Scholastic New Zealand Limited
Private Bag 94407, Botany, Manukau 2163, New Zealand

Scholastic Children's Books
Euston House, 24 Eversholt Street, London NW1 1DB, UK

www.scholastic.ca

Cover photograph © Tim Clayton/Corbis.

Library and Archives Canada Cataloguing in Publication

Carroll, David, 1966-
Ultra / by David Carroll.

Issued also in electronic format.
ISBN 978-1-4431-1918-4

I. Title.

PS8605.A77724U57 2013   jC813'.6   C2013-901815-8

6 5 4 3 2 1   Printed in Canada 121   13 14 15 16 17

MIX
Paper from
responsible sources
FSC® C004071

For Shawna.
And Mom and Dad.

THE STARTING LINE

Mile 0

QUINN: I still don't get why it was such a big deal. All kids like to run. Go to any schoolyard. You'll see kids playing tag, soccer, capture-the-flag . . . All those games involve running.

SYDNEY WATSON WALTERS: The difference is, most kids run for 10 or 15 minutes. Not for 24 hours straight, like you.

(Audience laughs)

QUINN: I still don't think I did anything special. My dad used to say, if you want to run an ultra-marathon, you have to be ultra tough, ultra fast and ultra determined. But I don't think I'm any of those things. Most of the time I was out there I just felt scared, slow and stupid.

SYDNEY WATSON WALTERS: Take me back to the starting line. That morning in July, before the race started. What was running through your head?

QUINN: I was thinking . . . I must be out of my mind.

"I can't believe you're doing this," Kneecap said. "Human beings aren't supposed to *run* a hundred miles. In a car, yes. On a bike, okay. But on two feet? That's just stupid. Stooooo-pid!"

Kneecap is my best friend in the world. Which isn't saying much, I guess, since she's my only friend.

"I mean, it's totally whacked!" she went on. "Running all day and all night, through a forest full of wild animals. You heard about the bears, right? Someone spotted a big one on the trail last night."

Mom overheard this. Her forehead crumpled like a plastic bag. She dug through her purse and handed me the phone. "Take it," she ordered.

"No way," I said. "It's too heavy."

"Not an option," Mom said.

I stared at the phone. Mom bought it a decade ago, when phones were as big as toaster ovens. When she just kept hanging on to it, Dad nicknamed it the Albatross.

"You do know I'm running a hundred miles, right?" I said.

"A little extra weight won't slow you down," said Mom.

"A *little*?" I said. "That thing weighs more than our fridge!"

It was 10 minutes before 6, and the sun was starting to come up. Seventy runners were milling up and down the dirt road, holding Styrofoam cups full of coffee and shivering. One woman rotated her arms like pinwheels; another pulled her ankle to her shoulder blade as if her leg were a noodle.

"If you want to run the race, you have to take the phone." Mom pressed the Albatross into my hand and shot me her death-ray stare.

I squeezed the phone into my fanny pack and struggled to zip it shut.

"Where's your brother?" Mom asked, glancing around.

I looked down the road. It was covered with shadows.

"There," said Kneecap.

In the half light, I could see Ollie standing at the edge of a ditch.

"He's getting his pyjamas wet," Mom sighed. "Quinn, would you go fish him out of there?"

I sloped down the road. A lineup of runners was standing beside a pair of portable toilets. A skinny lady in a baseball cap waved to me.

I caught up with Ollie. "What's going on?" I asked.

He was standing beside a creek, staring down at a clump of weeds. "There's a frog in there somewhere," he said.

I stared at the ground.

"Spring peeper?" I asked.

"Nope. Leopard frog."

We went on staring but couldn't see anything moving except a light breeze blowing through the grass.

"When does the race start?" Ollie asked.

"In ten minutes," I said, leaning over to stretch out my hamstrings. A wedge of yellow light was creeping over the foothills.

"Too bad Daddy isn't here to see this," Ollie said.

A huge raven, the size of a golden retriever, soared over the clearing. It screeched at us — a weird, lonely cry — and the loneliness grabbed me by the throat. My eyes started to burn, but I knew that I wouldn't cry. Not with Ollie there beside me.

"You'll be visiting the Shrine, right?" Ollie asked. "You promised Daddy you'd stop there, remember?"

I nodded and poked around inside my fanny pack. The photograph was still there, stowed in one pocket. My salt tablets and energy gels were in there too, plus the Albatross, of course.

"Don't forget your racing bib," Ollie said.

"Oh, right," I said. I knelt down so he could pin the number to my shirt.

"Isn't thirteen bad luck?" Ollie asked.

"Not for me it isn't," I said.

We finally got the number pinned on straight.

Ollie stepped back. "Knock knock," he said.

"Who's there?" I asked, rolling my eyes.

"Aardvark."

"Aardvark who?"

"Aardvark a hundred miles . . . for one of your smiles!"

A stupid joke. He'd heard it from my dad, the master of stupid knock-knock jokes. Dad had run this race before, and I knew he wished he could be running it again.

The blat of a bullhorn shattered the morning quiet: "ALL RUNNERS TO THE STARTING LINE!"

Electricity shot through my veins. "C'mon, we've got to go!" I said. Ollie and I jogged back toward the starting corral. All I could think was: I am about to run 100 miles.

Mom saw us coming and cleared a space in the crowd. She took Ollie's hand and brushed his bangs out of his eyes. "I thought we agreed you'd stay dry," she said.

Ollie kicked the road with the toe of his rubber boot. "But I was looking for frogs," he mumbled.

Kneecap appeared out of nowhere and slung her arm around his shoulder. "You're a *frogaholic*, Ollie."

Ollie giggled and pointed at my racing bib. "And you're a *jogaholic*!" he said.

I laughed at that. So did Mom. Kneecap punched me in the shoulder — hard.

"Ouch!" I said. "What was that for?"

"You laughed!" she said. "You actually laughed!"

"So what?" I said. "I laugh all the time."

"As *if*!" said Kneecap. "You used to laugh. Lately you've been a total fun vampire, sucking the fun out of everything."

I did?

The bullhorn boomed. "GOOOOD MORRRRRNING, ATHLETES!"

The crowd of runners spun around. Bruce, the race director, was standing beside the gatehouse. He was dressed in a plaid kilt and a black hoodie that said *Shin-Kicker 100* across the front. His head was shaved and he had mutton-chop sideburns. A rainbow-coloured scarf was wrapped around his throat.

"YOU RUNNERS ARE LOOKING STRONG!" he bellowed.

The runners cheered. Bruce raised a hairy arm in the air and then walked backward across the road, kicking a line in the dirt with the heel of his boot. "This is your new best friend," he announced. "It's the starting line *and* the finish line. Two minutes from now you'll cross this line. And in roughly twenty-four hours, if you're lucky, you'll cross it again, only by then you'll be a totally different person."

Kneecap punched me again. "You're really doing this!"

she said. "You're actually going to run a hundred miles!"

I didn't answer. I was still thinking: fun vampire?

"The thermometer's headed up to thirty-three degrees," Bruce went on, "so be sure to drink lots of liquids out there. We've got emergency water drops at miles nineteen and fifty-seven, just in case. If anyone gets heatstroke and ruins my race, I swear I'll feed you to the bears myself."

"See?" said Kneecap. "I *told* you there were bears."

Mom took my arm. "Quinn, are you sure you want to do this?" she said.

Stupid question. "Of course," I said.

Mom kept brushing Ollie's bangs with her fingers. "I'm just worried that people will think I'm irresponsible," she muttered. "You don't think I'm an irresponsible mother, do you?"

This was bad. She'd already cleared me for takeoff. I couldn't let her back out now.

"I'll be fine," I said firmly. "I've got superpowers, remember?"

"I know," said Mom. "But that won't help against the bears."

Kneecap stepped in. "Don't worry, Mrs. Scheurmann," she said. "The bears won't come anywhere near Quinn so long as he keeps singing. You can do that, can't you, Q-Tip? Sing some of your songs. That'll scare the bears off for sure."

"SIXTY SECONDS!" Bruce shouted into the bullhorn.

I clipped on my hydration pack and took a sip from my water bottle. The other runners peeled off their windbreakers and tearaway pants and lobbed them to the side of the trail. I suddenly needed to go to the bathroom, even though I'd gone 15 minutes before.

"Remember," Bruce said, his voice tinny and electric, "in every race there is a surprise."

Mom whispered into my ear, "What does that mean?"

"I don't know," I said.

"Excuse me!" Mom shouted. "What kind of surprise?"

We never found out, because Bruce began counting: "THIRTY! . . . TWENTY-NINE! . . . TWENTY-EIGHT! . . . TWENTY-SEVEN!"

"Twenty-six! . . . Twenty-five! . . . Twenty-four!" the runners chanted.

Kneecap pressed something into my hand. "Take this," she said.

It was her brand new phone. "I can't take that," I said.

"Sure you can," she said. "It's got GPS. It could save your life. Plus, it's lighter than your mom's piece of junk."

I looked over at my mom. She was chewing the ends of her hair. This race needed to start fast, before she changed her mind.

"But you love your phone," I said. "You'll go into withdrawal without it."

"It's only for twenty-four hours," said Kneecap.

"But — "

"Shut up and take it," she said. She reached out and grabbed the Albatross out of my pouch and tucked her phone back in its place. "Please don't get it wet," she said.

I nodded and tugged the zipper closed.

"TEN! . . . NINE! . . . EIGHT!"

I stretched my legs one last time.

"SEVEN! . . . SIX! . . . FIVE!"

Took one last sip of water.

"FOUR! . . . THREE! . . . TWO!"

Stole one last glance at Mom.

The gun exploded. "GO!"

One hundred miles. 160 kilometres. Half a million strides. Starting NOW.

I took my first step. It would be hours before I reached the first rest stop, and two sunrises before I'd cross the finish line — if I crossed it at all.

"Yaaaaaaaaaaaaaaaaaaaaa!" the runners shouted.

I took a second step. And then a third. People on the sidelines cheered.

I was about to burn 10,000 calories. Sweat 20 litres of water. My heart would beat 1.2 million times.

I took a fourth stride. And then a fifth. And after I had taken a fifth, there was nothing to do but take a sixth. I'd travelled 4 whole metres already! Only 159,996 to go.

I jogged down the trail with the rest of the runners. Ollie ran beside me. "Good luck!" he shouted.

He twirled his pyjama top above his head. My lunatic little brother. My good-luck charm.

I waved back at Mom. Her face was a sinking ship.

"Go for it, buddy!" Kneecap shouted. "Kick some shins!"

HOW I GOT
MY SUPERPOWERS

SYDNEY WATSON WALTERS: So let's discuss this superhero business. In her White House blog, Michelle Obama called you a superhero.

QUINN: That's a nice way of putting it. Most kids at my school think I'm a super-freak.

SYDNEY WATSON WALTERS: They're just jealous of what you've done.

QUINN: I doubt it. Ultra-marathoning is about as cool as log-rolling. Nobody's lining up for my autograph, that's for sure.

SYDNEY WATSON WALTERS: We should explain. For those viewers who may not know, ultra-marathoning is when people run any distance that's longer than a traditional marathon, which is 26 miles, or 42 kilometres. Is that correct?

QUINN: Exactly.

SYDNEY WATSON WALTERS: And you were running a really long ultra — 100 miles. How do you train for a race like that?

QUINN: I ran for 2 hours almost every day. I'd run to school in the morning and then back home in the afternoon. Tuesday and Thursday nights I also ran my flyer route. And every Saturday I ran to Kendra Station for my piano lesson.

SYDNEY WATSON WALTERS: How many miles were you running every week?

QUINN: A hundred, maybe a hundred and ten. I wore out three pairs of running shoes in four months.

SYDNEY WATSON WALTERS: I've heard that your body is different from most people's.

QUINN: Yeah, my heart is freakishly big. Twenty per cent bigger than other kids my age.

SYDNEY WATSON WALTERS: How does that affect your running?

QUINN: A bigger heart can pump more blood. The more blood your heart pumps, the more oxygen gets delivered to your muscles, and the easier it is to run. So I don't tire out as fast as other runners. Plus, I have another advantage.

SYDNEY WATSON WALTERS: I've heard about this — your body doesn't produce much lactic acid, right?

QUINN: Exactly. You know how, when you run really hard, your legs start to burn? That's the lactic acid. It fills up your muscles and slows you down. But my body sucks at making the stuff. So I can run for a really long time without conking out.

SYDNEY WATSON WALTERS: When did you realize that you had these superpowers?

QUINN: A long time ago . . .

I was eight. Dad was training for a marathon that spring, and every morning he'd get up early for a jog. One day he caught me watching cartoons. "Hey, Quinn, want to come?" he asked. .

"No thanks," I said. Why run when I could sit? That was how I thought back then.

"Come on," he said. "Quality time with your dad! We never get to hang out, just you and me."

This was true. Oliver was still a baby then, and between the feedings and diaper changings he was hogging my mom and dad all to himself.

"Come on," Dad said. "I'm just doing one loop of the Headwaters Trail. You can run it faster than me, I bet."

I tossed on my gym shorts and my Oilers jersey. I didn't have any real running shoes then, so I just pulled on my Wheelies. Dad and I crept out the back door without waking Mom or Ollie, and then we crossed the field behind our house and jogged up Appleby Line.

It was a crisp April morning, and the trees were covered with lime-green buds. The sky was as blue as a swimming pool.

"I'm cold," I said. "Can I go back for my jacket?"

"You won't need it," said Dad. "We'll be sweating in no time."

The trailhead appeared at the end of the subdivision. We trotted down the path in single file, skirting the little creek that leads to Watson's Pond.

"Don't go too fast," Dad called out. "Save some energy for later."

I sprinted ahead, to show him who was boss. No one else was on the trail, and I sang out loudly as I ran.

You got bike spokes in your stomach
And your veins are full of stones
And did you need to fill your 'hood
With all those broken bones?

It was a song by Troutspawn, one of my dad's favourite bands. Troutspawn was one of my favourite bands too.

The dirt path led up the side of the hill. I charged up the slope until I saw a stripe of orange. I stopped and looked down. Hundreds of caterpillars were crawling around in every direction.

"Woolly bears," Dad said, pulling up behind me. "Skunks love to eat those guys."

"Really?" I asked.

"Sure. The skunks roll them over and over on the ground, until they scrape off all the long hairs."

The caterpillars pulsed slowly along. I imagined the skunks rolling them in the dirt as if they were pizza dough, then chewing them into ribbons of goo. "Not a very nice way to die," I said.

"That's Mother Nature for you," said Dad.

We started running again. The hillside was covered in trilliums and forget-me-nots. The path got steep, and when I stopped and looked behind me, I couldn't see my dad anymore. I figured he must have stopped to walk.

At the top of the hill, the trail popped out of the woods and crossed a grassy field. A little stone church stood not far away. I jogged over to the graveyard and sat down on a wooden bench to wait for Dad. He appeared a few minutes later. He was gasping for air and his face was bright red. He sat down on the bench, rubbing his knee.

"That's a tough little hill," he said.

"I guess so," I said. I didn't think it was that tough.

I walked over to the edge of the escarpment. Kneecap calls Tudhope a "flyspeck town," but it looked sort of pretty from up here. I could see the water tower with the name of our town in block letters, and the empty parking lot where the bus stops six times a week. I could see the marina docks where, in another couple of months, the motor boats would be tied up.

I jogged back over to my dad. "Running's really easy!" I said.

He smiled and went on rubbing his leg. "Told you it was fun," he said.

My dad didn't look like your typical runner. He had thick, short legs and a bit of a pot belly. He was five foot eleven and he weighed two hundred pounds. Most of that was muscle, though.

"Ready to run back down?" he asked.

"Of course!" I said.

Dad pulled himself to his feet and stretched his arms above his head. "Tell me if your legs start to burn," he said. "We can always slow down and walk."

It was a billion times more fun running down than climbing up. I thumped down the path, taking huge leaping strides, and at times it felt like I was flying. At a bend in the trail, I jumped over a pile of pebbly deer turds. I let out a yodel and I could hear Dad yodelling behind me. The scent of moss and mud filled my nostrils, and soon we were back at the bottom of the hill.

Suddenly, I heard a noise. *Rat-a-tat-a-tat!*

It was Dad, behind me. He was farting. Popcorn farts.
Rat-a-TAT-TAT! Rat-a-TAT-TAT!

He farted with every step. It must have gone on for 30 seconds.

"Quinn!" said Dad. "Excuse yourself!"

The path rounded Watson's Pond and led us back to Appleby Line. Kneecap waved from a few doors down.

"Yo, Quinn!" she shouted. "Hey, Mr. Scheurmann."

She was standing in her driveway, shooting baskets. We bounded over.

"What's going on?" Kneecap asked.

"We're running!" I said.

"How far did you go?"

"Four kilometres," said Dad. "Two going up and another two coming down."

He'd stopped farting, which was a good thing.

I wasn't tired at all. "Let's do it again!" I said.

Dad raised one eyebrow.

Kneecap pointed at my feet. "Shouldn't you wear some *real* shoes?" she asked.

Dad started to laugh. "You ran in *those*?" he said. "But they have wheels!"

I blushed and ran into Kneecap's house, shouted hi to her mom, and yanked on a pair of Kneecap's trainers. She and I had the same size feet. I came back outside and shouted, "I'm good. Let's go!"

We began our second loop at 9:22 a.m.

Kneecap ran a clock on us. "Thirty-three minutes and thirty-six seconds," she announced when we got back.

"Not bad," said Dad.

14

"Again!" I said.

Our third loop was faster. 29:06.

"Pretty good," said Dad.

"Again!" I said.

As we ran, Dad told stupid jokes.

"What happens when you double-park your frog?" he asked.

"I don't know," I replied.

"It gets toad!"

Mason Pond appeared around the bend. Turtles were sunning themselves on bone-coloured logs.

"What's the difference between roast beef and pea soup?" Dad asked.

"Tell me," I said.

"Anyone can roast beef!"

While we ran, Dad peeled off his shirt. Yeah, he was one of those no-shirt dads. Mom hated it when he ran bare-chested; she was always chasing after him with a bottle of sunscreen.

"Talk to me, Quinn," he said. "It's your turn to tell a joke. Better yet, tell me a story."

I told him about school, about my teachers, about exponents.

"Tell me about that girl," he said.

"Who? Kneecap?"

"Yeah. What kind of a name is that?"

I told him the story behind her name. He laughed and told me about all the nicknames he'd had. His friends had called him Pickles, Socks, Bubbles, even Floater. He hadn't liked any of them. There was only one nickname he'd liked.

"Seriously?" I said. "Those guys call you Yoda?"

"That's right," he said.

"But why?" I asked.

"Because sometimes, even though I'm just a grunt, I actually say some pretty smart things. And even though I'm slow and fat, I can still kick butt when the going gets tough."

Our fourth loop sucked. We ran it in 34:20. I could have gone faster, but Dad was losing steam.

"Again!" I said.

Dad grimaced. "Aren't you tired?" he said.

"Nope!"

It was weird: the longer we ran, the stronger I felt.

The fifth loop was our fastest yet: 27 minutes, 40 seconds. When we finished, Dad lay down on the driveway.

"I am totally done!" he said. "No, Quinn, I am *not* running another loop!"

Kneecap's mom gave us kiwi juice and toasted bagels. Dad stood up and stretched his legs. His left hip made a gruesome clicking noise.

"Ew!" Kneecap cried. "That's disgusting!"

Dad stretched it again. "What, this?" he asked.

Later, when we got home, I told Mom how far I'd run. She didn't react the way I expected.

"You can wreck your own knees for all I care!" she told my dad. "But don't wreck his! He's just a kid!"

"But you should see him run," Dad said. "We ran for three hours and he wasn't even tired!"

This was a tactical mistake. "You made him run for three *hours*?" Mom cried.

A couple of weeks later, Dad took me to a special clinic.

They put me on a treadmill and took about a hundred vials of my blood. Two weeks later the results came back.

"It's confirmed," Dad said. "What colour cape do you want?"

GOING, GOING, GONE
Mile 1

SYDNEY WATSON WALTERS: So let's get back to the 100-mile race. You'd just started running. You were about to *kick some shins!*

QUINN: Right. There were seventy-seven runners in the race. And the trail was only a metre wide, so it was a traffic jam at first. All I could hear was the sound of seventy-seven pairs of sneakers slapping the dirt, and the sloshing of water in seventy-seven hydration packs, and the farts of seventy-six middle-aged long-distance runners. Luckily the pack spread out pretty quickly. The greyhounds zipped off, and the slowpokes fell behind, and soon we were all stretched out in a long, thin line.

SYDNEY WATSON WALTERS: And how were you feeling?

QUINN: Pretty good, except I had a knot in my stomach. Plus, I was still mad at Kneecap.

SYDNEY WATSON WALTERS: Because of what she said to you?

QUINN: Yeah. *Fun vampire.* It's not exactly a compliment.

Still, I was happy to be out there running. The sky was pink, and the air smelled of damp wood. The forest was full of all these golden stripes of sunlight. Tiny birds were zinging between the trees.

After about 10 minutes we passed a red signpost. Mile 1, the sign said.

"Only ninety-nine to go!" someone shouted.

"This isn't so hard after all," said someone else.

I was running behind a group of grey-haired men. They laughed and horked up gobs of phlegm and bragged about all the races they'd run.

They also talked a lot about body functions. Like, Hey, Bob, did you have a bowel movement this morning? Yeah, Steve, I had three! Wow, lucky you! I guess today's gonna be a fertilizer run, huh?

(Pause)

QUINN: Oh, wait; you probably don't want to hear this, do you?

SYDNEY WATSON WALTERS: I'm not sure our national audience wants to hear about bowel movements, no.

(Audience laughs)

Quinn, I'm still trying to understand how anyone can run 100 miles. I mean, that's like running four full marathons, back to back. I know you have superpowers, but . . . And how did you keep from getting bored? Did you listen to music along the way?

QUINN: No, but I sang a lot.

SYDNEY WATSON WALTERS: What did you sing?

QUINN: My own songs, mostly. I'm a songwriter. I've written ninety-three songs so far. I can play some of them on piano; others I just keep in my head. I'm always singing them, even though I'm not a very good singer.

SYDNEY WATSON WALTERS: So singing helps you relax? What about running — does that help you relax too?

QUINN: Yeah. It quiets down my brain, you know? My brain is always screaming crazy stuff at me. Like, when I walk down the hallway at school, it tells me that my clothes look stupid, or that everyone hates my guts.

But that's nothing compared to what happens at night. My brain gets really noisy then. I'll be lying in bed, thinking I want a glass of water. But then my brain will tell me that if I open my bedroom door, my mom will disappear and I won't see her again. I know it's crazy, since I can hear my mom watching TV. Still, for some reason, I can't open my bedroom door.

But when I run, my brain quiets down. The longer I run, the quieter it gets.

SYDNEY WATSON WALTERS: It's like taking a vacation from yourself?

QUINN: Yeah, it can be pretty exhausting, being me.

Anyway, the race. I was still running behind those phlegmy old guys. After a while they started talking about interest rates and mortgages, so I thought, Screw this, I'm outta here!

I put on some speed and left them in the dust. By the time I hit the Mile 2 signpost, I was running on my own.

Kneecap's phone vibrated. I pulled it out of my fanny pack as I ran. Ollie had texted me: GO QUINN GO!

Suddenly, I heard footsteps. "On your left!" a voice called out. A skinny man with wispy grey hair flew by.

"Nice pace," he said out of the side of his mouth. It sounded like a sneer.

He was wearing a black T-shirt with the words *Eat My Dirt!* on the back. And striped neon-green socks pulled up to his knees. The socks looked ridiculous, and I was about to laugh, but then the guy stopped running and turned around.

"Hey, you," he said. "What's your name?"

"Quinn," I said.

He had hollow cheeks and porridgy legs. He looked as though he'd drunk a mouthful of sour milk.

"You shouldn't be out here," he said. "You're just a kid."

I stared at him and said nothing. He stared back. He was serious.

"Your parents must be crazy," he said. "This race is too dangerous for someone your age."

I crossed my arms over my chest.

Mr. Eat My Dirt scowled. "Do yourself a favour and drop out at Silver Valley," he muttered.

Silver Valley, at Mile 22, was the first rest stop. No way was I going to drop out there.

"Take my advice," he said. "You're not cut out for this race." Then he spun around and started running again.

I hate being passed, especially by crusty old men, so I chased Mr. Dirt Eater down the ravine. My heart was hammering, partly from the running, but mostly because I was really mad! What kind of creep would tell me to drop out?

Unfortunately, as hard as I tried to hold the pace, Mr. Dirt Eater was just too fast. For a while I could see him ahead of me, but then his neon socks disappeared around a bend in the trail.

Break time, I thought. I slowed to a walk and pulled out my bottle. It held 750 millilitres of water, plus I had 3 litres more in my hydration pack. Hopefully, that would last me until Silver Valley.

The sun was really coming up now. The ground was a mess of dead leaves and pine needles, which had dried up and turned the colour of rust.

I stuffed my water bottle back into its holster and started running again. The trail bobbed up and down like a roller coaster, and I figured I was headed north, since the sun was to my right. The sun followed me sideways as I ran, until it disappeared behind Chimney Top Mountain. A little stream ran beside the trail, and I figured it was taking me to Hither Lake. Hither Lake was huge — almost 50 kilometres long — and over the next 24 hours, I was going to run all the way around it.

Hopefully.

Another signpost: Mile 3. Around this time I started to sing. I sang one of the first songs I ever wrote, a song called "Run Baby Run."

> *What he's running from —*
> *To himself he doesn't show.*
> *And what he's running to*
> *Even he doesn't know.*

Suddenly I heard a jingling sound. I spun around and saw a woman in a baseball cap. Her skin was walnut brown, and her face was freckled. She was as thin as a cedar sapling.

"Hey there," she said. "How's it going?"

"Not bad," I said.

She ran up beside me and flashed a warm smile. It was the lady who'd been in line outside the portable toilets.

"Hey, you're just a kid," she said.

"Actually, I'm a teenager," I said.

"You're tearing up the trail, that's for sure," she said.

A little bell was tied to one of her shoes.

"What's that for?" I asked.

"It scares the bears away," she said.

"Bears are scared of bells?" I asked.

"Black bears are scared of *everything*."

She stopped running and scrambled down to the little stream. "Hang on for just a second, okay?" she said.

She splashed water on her face and tightened her shoelaces. Then she climbed back up to the trail.

"What's your goal?" she asked.

"I'm not sure," I said. "I guess I'd like to break twenty-four hours."

My dad always dreamed of breaking 24 hours in this race, but he'd never come anywhere close.

The tanned lady checked her watch and nodded. "You're right on pace."

We started running again.

"Are you in the forces?" I asked. I'd recognized the tattoo on her calf.

"No, I'm a cop."

"Oh," I said. "Cool."

Stupidest word in the English language, *cool*. But I couldn't think of anything else to say.

"I'm Kara," the woman said.

"I'm Quinn."

We fist-bumped.

"Is this your first ultra?" she asked.

I told her yes.

"You're gonna love it," she said. "The mountains, the lakes. This whole course is awesome possum."

Her face was the shape of a bicycle seat. Round at the top, with a pointy chin. She looked like a character from my favourite video game, except that she didn't have the animal ears.

"Have you run this race before?" I asked.

"Yeah, I won it last year," she said.

"Seriously?"

"It took me twenty-one hours," Kara said. "But I got lost along the way. I ran four extra miles by mistake."

She smiled to think of it and then she glanced at her watch. "Come on," she said, "let's make some time."

With that, she blasted down the path — light years faster than I'd been running before. Thank God for all those training runs with my dad because this lady liked to run *fast*!

The trail narrowed and the forest closed in around us. Suddenly it felt like we were running through a tunnel. Dead trees had fallen across the path, and sharp branches stuck out in all directions. Kara held back the branches so they wouldn't slap my face. I thought that was pretty cool of her.

One time we came to an old, dead log. I tried to jump over it, but that was a mistake. When I landed, my ankle folded like a soggy piece of pizza.

"Frick!" I yelped. A spear of white-hot pain shot up my leg. It felt like I'd landed on a barbecue skewer.

Twisted ankle for sure, I thought, or a broken shin. Or maybe I'd snapped my Achilles tendon!

I hopped for a few steps. Belted out a few more swear words.

Kara stopped running and turned around. "Quinn, are you okay?" she said.

My eyes were watering, and I could barely breathe. I coughed a couple of times and leaned against a tree. "I'm good," I sputtered. "Awesome possum."

Slowly, I put my injured foot back on the ground. Then a miracle happened. I took a couple of steps. The pain was mostly gone.

"I was sure I'd twisted it," I said.

Kara knelt down and pressed both sides of my ankle. She carefully bent my foot back and forth.

"It's your lucky day," she said. "But watch your step. It's too early in the race to get an injury."

We walked for a few minutes, following the creek, which tumbled down a series of rocky waterfalls. I picked my way down the steep hill, dodging tree stumps and boulders, at a cautious speed.

"If you hurt yourself later, that's not so bad," said Kara. "But you want to get sixty or seventy miles under your belt. That way, even if you get a DNF, your friends will still be impressed by how far you got."

I sure wasn't going to settle for a Did Not Finish in my first ultra. So we started running again.

A few minutes later another runner came into view. I recognized the T-shirt and the neon socks instantly. He wasn't going nearly as fast as before.

"Looking good!" I shouted as we flew past.

The Dirt Eater said nothing, but I heard him spit into the forest. I had the feeling I'd see him again.

Kara and I ground our way up another hill. We popped out on a narrow ridge and I was blinded by the sun.

"Watch your step here," Kara said.

Thirty metres below, waves crashed against rocks. Hither Lake spread out before us.

"Isn't it gorgeous?" Kara shouted back to me.

Parts of the lake were the colour of strawberry milk, and other parts looked like crinkled tinfoil.

"This is my church," Kara shouted over the gusts of wind. "I was raised Presbyterian, but now I worship Mother Nature. This is God we're running on. We're running across her back."

I pulled my sunglasses down over my eyes. The lake was frosted with whitecaps, and little boats rolled on top of the waves. The breeze slapped my face and made my eyes water. Kara was running faster than ever, and I had to concentrate to keep from falling off the cliff.

Suddenly Kara's phone rang. Great, I thought. She'll slow down and walk. But Kara had no intention of slowing down. She just yakked away while she sprinted down the trail.

"Hi, honey!" she said. "Did you get your breakfast? Don't forget to have some fruit, okay? There are oranges in the fridge."

Seagulls flew above us, screeching loudly. It sounded like they were yelling, "T-shirt! T-shirt!"

There was a pause. Then Kara said, "You called to ask

me *that*? You know what my answer is. Give the controller to your sister."

Kara was running too fast for me. I was gasping for breath, and I was on the verge of launching lunch.

SYDNEY WATSON WALTERS: Wait a second, Quinn. I'm not following. You said that you had superpowers. How could Kara leave you in her dust?

QUINN: My superpowers make it easy for me to run for a *long* time. But I'm no good at running fast. I'm what they call *slow and steady*. Kara really was getting a long way ahead — even while she was talking to her kids.

But eventually Kara ended her call. "Sorry," she shouted back. "That was my son. He and his sister aren't exactly getting along."

"Can . . . we . . . slow . . . down . . . a . . . bit?" I gasped.

"What's that?" said Kara.

I could barely breathe, let alone speak.

"Can . . . we . . . slow . . . down?" I repeated.

"Sure, why didn't you say so?"

She dialed it right back. A good thing too. I was about to blow biscuits all over the trail.

I bent over and swallowed air. Kara stared at her watch.

"Don't wait for me," I said.

"I don't mind," she said. "We're still ahead of pace. No point in going out too fast."

She walked along the trail ahead of me. The clouds slid across the sky like they were being pulled by strings. I stared at the lake. It was as big as an ocean. You could barely see the other side.

"We're running all the way around *that*?" I said.

"If we're lucky," said Kara. "Hey, did you bring any drop bags?"

I nodded to Kara. I'd packed two of them, each waterproof and stuffed with food and extra gear. Mom was delivering them to the rest stops farther on.

"How about extra clothes?" she asked.

"I packed a windbreaker, tights and gloves."

Kara gave me a thumbs-up. "You're in good shape then. It can get cold out here at night, but if you've got gloves, you'll be fine."

Soon, we came to a wooden staircase. It led us down to a pebble beach. I needed a break, so I picked up a flat stone and flung it into the lake. I tried to make it skip, but it landed in the water with a disappointing *plop*.

Kara threw a stone and it skipped ten times.

"How old are your kids?" I asked her.

"Grace is seven. Jackson's nine."

"Are they coming out to cheer you on?"

"Nah," said Kara. "They came to my races when they were younger, but now they prefer to stay home and beat each other up."

The sun came out from behind a cloud. It spread its warm, liquid rays across the beach. I leaned over to stretch out my back, opened a banana-flavoured gel and squeezed the sugary goo into my mouth.

"Have you got a pacer?" Kara asked.

I knew I should have. When it's dark and cold and you've

already run 70 miles, it's nice to have someone running with you those last 30. But no, I didn't have a pacer.

"I don't have one either," said Kara. "Who knows, maybe you and I can pace each other. If we're still running together later tonight, that is."

"Won't happen," I said, squirting water into my mouth and swishing it around with the sweet syrup. "I'm nowhere near as fast as you."

"Not right now, you're not," Kara agreed. "But anything can happen. A hundred miles is a long way."

She bent over and whipped another stone at the lake. It skipped fifteen times. The lady was good!

"In the hundred-mile race, we don't compete against other people," I said. "We only compete against ourselves."

Kara grinned like a sunlamp. "Who fed you that pile of baloney?" she asked.

"My dad," I said.

She shook her head, still laughing. "You can cling to that if you want," she said. "It might help you feel better when I kick your butt!"

With that, we started running again, following the trail up the bluff and back into the woods. Kara threaded a course between dead stumps and fallen logs, and I followed behind, watching her ponytail bounce back and forth. My stomach felt better, and for a while I didn't notice that the gap between the two of us was growing. But soon I couldn't read the letters on Kara's shirt, and the jingling of her bell became very faint. Then she was just a splash of colour far down the trail. Finally she rounded a bend and disappeared.

FINDING MY PACER
Mile 7

SYDNEY WATSON WALTERS: So how far had you run by this time? Five or six miles?

QUINN: Seven. Which meant the first rest stop, the one at Silver Valley, was still 15 miles away.

SYDNEY WATSON WALTERS: Did you run all that way by yourself?

QUINN: Yeah, but I was okay with that. I don't need to be around other people all the time. My dad always liked running with other people, but I'm usually pretty happy on my own. Besides, I had Kneecap's phone.

Around Mile 10, I called the Albatross. Kneecap answered.

"Hey, Q-Tip!" she said.

"What's going on?" I said.

"Not much," said Kneecap. "How's my phone?"

"Actually," I said, "I was drinking some Gatorade and, well . . . I had a bit of an accident . . . "

"What?" she cried. "You promised you'd take care — "

I held my tongue. There was a delicious pause.

"Ah," she said, clueing in. "Nice one, Scheurmann."

"Gotcha," I said.

"You're a freak," she said. "You know that?"

"Better than being a fun vampire," I shot back.

There was a moment's pause. Then Kneecap spoke: "You know that I meant that in a good way, right?" she said. "You aren't a fun vampire anymore. You're getting a lot better!"

I looked at the ground and didn't say anything. Tiny red flowers were growing along the edge of the trail.

"How far have you run?" Kneecap asked.

"Almost ten miles," I said. "I'm at Leaning Pine Point."

"Not bad," she said. "And you've only been running for two hours. At that pace you should be finished by . . . let me see . . . Thanksgiving!"

She was eating something. I could hear chewing noises. "What are you stuffing your face with?" I asked.

"Only the best food ever," Kneecap said.

"Banana?"

"You got it."

She took another bite and smacked her lips. It was pretty gross, I have to say.

"Is Ollie there?" I asked.

"Hang on a sec." I heard muffled voices and banging metal. Pocket-call garble: "Hey, Ollie! You in there?"

Another bang. Then, footsteps on gravel.

"Ew!" Kneecap shouted. "Ick factor six!"

There was a clacking sound and then a very loud hiss. At last, Ollie's voice came on the line.

"Hello?" he said.

"Hey, Ollie," I said. "Where *are* you?"

"In the bathroom," said Ollie. "Sitting on the toilet."

Totally *not* what I expected to hear.

"No," I said. "I mean, where are you, on a map?"

"Silver Valley," said Ollie. "We just dropped off your bags. They tied them onto the back of a horse."

"Really?" I said.

"Yeah. His name is Mercury. I don't think they tied the bags on tight enough, though."

I could hear the squeak of a toilet-paper dispenser, and I knew instantly what my brother was up to — unspooling a mountain of toilet paper on to the floor. He was always getting into trouble for it at home.

"I won't be there for two more hours," I said. "I hope you don't mind waiting a bit."

"That's okay," he said. "Mom's taking us to an antique shop."

"Sorry to hear that," I said. "But listen, I need your help."

A spiderweb broke across my face as I walked down the path.

"What kind of help?" Ollie asked.

"I need you to be my pacer," I said, rubbing the web off the bridge of my nose.

"What's a pacer?"

"Whenever I hit a rough patch," I said, "like if I run out of energy, or lose my way, I'll give you a call on the phone."

"And then what am I supposed to do?"

"Tell me a joke or a story," I said. "Do whatever it takes to cheer me up."

Ollie was silent at the other end of the line.

"Can you do that?" I asked.

"I think so." He sounded uncertain. "But why me?"

"Because we're a team," I said. "Don't you remember? That time you and I went running together?"

"We ran together?" said Ollie.

"We sure did," I said. "But you were only two, so you probably won't remember."

Dad was away, and Mom had a cold, so one night I had to feed him and put him to bed. I gave him a bowl of macaroni and cheese, and then we watched an episode of *Wallace and Gromit*.

"I remember that show!" said Ollie. "Which episode did we watch? 'The Wrong Trousers'?"

"I can't remember," I said. "After dinner we danced around to Dad's Troutspawn CDs and then we read *The Pop-Up Truck Book*. Finally, at nine-thirty, I put you to bed. But you were totally wired and refused to go to sleep."

"You should've read me *The Velveteen Rabbit*," said Ollie.

"I did," I said. "But that didn't help either. You asked where Daddy had gone, so I told you. Then you started to cry. I was scared you'd wake Mom, so I dressed you in your winter clothes, clipped you into your stroller and took you outside for a run. We ran all the way to Eugenia Line and back."

"Eugenia Line?" said Ollie. "That's really far!"

"I know," I said.

"Was it dark out?" Ollie asked.

"What do you think? It was eleven at night. It was darker than Darth Vader's helmet."

"Did I fall asleep in the stroller?"

"Yep. You were out in thirty seconds."

An inchworm appeared in front of my nose. It was parachuting down from a tree above. I reached out and caught it on the tip of my finger.

"Did we get caught?" Ollie asked.

"Nope," I said. "Mom slept through the whole thing. She'd have stuffed my running shoes in the food processor if she'd found out."

The inchworm crawled up the length of my finger. I knelt down and coaxed it onto a pine cone beside the trail.

"Anyway," I said, "that was the first time I ran at night. And you were right there with me."

Just then I heard another runner approaching. I expected to see the Dirt Eater, but instead it was a skinny woman wearing a shirt that looked like the Jamaican flag. She wore a skirt instead of shorts and very cool bug-eyed sunglasses. She waved as she zipped by, then disappeared down the trail.

"I really need your help tonight," I told Ollie. "You have to promise me one thing. Promise you won't let me drop out of the race."

The trees around me trembled in the breeze. Ninety more miles, I thought. What had Dad been thinking when he let me sign up?

"No matter what happens, you can't let me flake out," I told Ollie. "Even if I have two broken feet, okay?"

"Okay," Ollie said. "I promise."

"Good," I said. "I've got to go. I'll see you when I get — "

"Wait! Don't you want to hear a joke?"

"Depends," I said. "Is it a knock-knock joke?"

"Yeah."

"Uh, I don't really have time . . . "

"Knock knock!" said Ollie.

"Who's there?" I said.

"Cows go."

It was one of Dad's old jokes. I'd heard it a million times before. But I decided to play along. "Cows go who?" I said.

"No they don't! Cows go *moo!*" Ollie squealed with laughter — a puppy with a chew toy.

I reached into my fanny pack to make sure the picture was still there. I pulled it out and looked at it for a few seconds. "Quinn, you still there?" Ollie asked.

"Yep," I said, stuffing the picture back into my pouch.

"That's good," said Ollie. "I have to hang up. It's time for me to wipe. Watch out for the bears!"

NOTHING
IS IMPOSSIBLE

SYDNEY WATSON WALTERS: We haven't talked much about your mom. How does she feel about your running?

QUINN: She's not too thrilled about it. She *definitely* didn't want me to sign up for the 100-mile race.

SYDNEY WATSON WALTERS: Hard to blame her. It's pretty extreme.

QUINN: Sure, I get that. And Mom's kind of nervous to begin with. If some people have an anxiety disorder, my mom has an anxiety volcano.

(Audience laughs)

SYDNEY WATSON WALTERS: You've received a lot of media attention since running the race. What has that been like for your mom?

QUINN: It's been hard on her. People have said some cruel things.

SYDNEY WATSON WALTERS: Really? Like what?

QUINN: Some guy on the radio said she's guilty of child abuse. He said Family Services should pay us a visit.

SYDNEY WATSON WALTERS: But it wasn't your mom who signed you up for the race. That was your dad's idea, wasn't it?

QUINN: Yeah. He'd run the Shin-Kicker a few times himself and he thought it would be cool if we ran it together. So last October he sent me the money so I could register. Mom nearly had a coronary over that, which is why Dad took me to a sports doctor and got me checked out.

The doctor said I was the fittest kid he'd ever seen. And that my diet is excellent, and I have no body fat to speak of.

Mom asked if the running would harm my knees.

The doctor said that a hundred miles is a ridiculous distance, but that I'd probably quit when it started to hurt.

I can still remember the look on my mom's face when the doctor said that. She knew she'd lost the battle, and her smile snapped like an old crayon. After that, she didn't ever ask about my running. But Dad and I talked about it all the time.

SYDNEY WATSON WALTERS: Did you and your dad do much training together?

QUINN: Lots. One time we drove out to Hither Lake and climbed all the way up Chimney Top Mountain. Dad said if I could conquer Chimney Top, then I was capable of anything. He was wrong about that, there are plenty of harder things, but Chimney Top was still a good place to train.

Chimney Top has this crazy, unmistakable shape. It rises out of the ground like a regular mountain, but two-thirds of the way up it flattens out, like someone smacked it with a fly swatter. It's a thousand metres tall, which is almost like two CN Towers stacked on top of each other. I just about died the first time I saw it.

"You want me to run up *that*?" I asked.

Dad grinned and nodded. "It's not that bad," he said. "Besides, you've got superpowers, remember?"

Hold out your index finger. Point it at the sun. Now, imagine running up your finger, only it's 6 kilometres long. The trail doesn't go straight up to the top, of course — there are plenty of hoodoos and switchbacks you have to hike around.

"You've gotta be kidding," I said, staring through the windshield. "That's impossible. You're crazy."

"Oh, come on," said Dad. "You've jumped ramps on your BMX bigger than this! When you were a baby, you took craps that were bigger!"

Dad parked the car at the foot of the mountain. We jogged to the trailhead in spitting rain.

"Hey now, look at that," said Dad. He pointed out a black pile of dung on the ground. It was the size of a hubcap.

"A bear did that?" I asked.

"A big one, yeah. There are his tracks, see?"

He showed me the footprints. I felt my guts turn to water.

"Don't worry," said Dad. "He's more afraid of us than we are of him."

"Really?" I said.

"You bet," said Dad. "Besides, bears are mostly vegetarian."

Mostly. That made me laugh. If bears are mostly vegetarian, what are they the rest of the time?

We started up the mountain. We jogged for a while; then,

when it got steeper, we power-walked. As we climbed, the hills in the distance seemed to be climbing too, and when we came to a lookout, the highway seemed really tiny below us.

"We're really climbing a mountain!" I said.

"Not yet," said Dad. "We're only on the apron."

A few minutes later we climbed into cloud. The world around us became grey and dim. Later we sidestepped some narrow ruts. "Mountain bikers were here," I said.

"No," said Dad. "That's a hoop-snake track."

"A what?" I said.

"You don't know about hoop snakes?" Dad said. "Awful things, terribly poisonous. They grab their tail in their mouth and roll down the hill like a bicycle tire. Scientists have clocked them doing a hundred kilometres an hour."

"You're a big fat liar," I said.

"I resent that," said Dad. "I'm not fat."

I was never sure when to believe my dad. He knew a lot about animals, especially whales, but sometimes he said things that didn't sound quite right. Like once, when I was little, I asked him how he'd lost all his hair. He thought about the question for a moment, as if deciding which version of the story he ought to tell.

"One day I was cooling off in Watson's Pond," he said finally, "and I must have swum too close to a beaver lodge, because WHAMMO, Mama Beaver appeared out of nowhere and went all shock-and-awe on my head! You know how beavers have those flat tails? Those things are as hard as a frying pan. My concussion was so bad, people called me Eric Lindros. And a couple of weeks later, all my hair fell out!"

This seemed to me a reasonable answer, until a month later I asked my dad the exact same question and got a completely different story.

"My hair?" said Dad. "Didn't I tell you about that? I was hiking in the forest and I came across a wolverine. He was a monster, claws as big as dinner knives. He took a swat at my throat, but I ducked sideways. Unfortunately, he caught the end of my ponytail."

In this version of the story, Mom fought off the wolverine with a pool noodle.

"A pool noodle!" I shrieked. "Mom, is that true?"

Mom smiled and shrugged her shoulders and disappeared into the kitchen.

"Of course it's true," Dad insisted. "Your father wouldn't tell you a lie, now would he?"

Good question.

We left the hoop-snake tracks behind and continued up the mountain.

The mist thinned out, and a ghostly curtain of rock appeared above us. Dad wiped the sweat off the back of his neck. "This is the same trail we'll follow in the Shin-Kicker," he said.

"Is Chimney Top really the hardest part of the race?" I asked.

"No, not really," Dad said.

"What's the hardest part?"

"The trail demons."

"Trail demons?" I asked.

Dad leaned against a boulder and took a sip from his water bottle. "When you run long distances, your brain gets really tired and it plays tricks on you to stop you from running."

"What kind of tricks?" I said.

The mist rolled back in, pressing against the granite cliffs like rumpled bedsheets. "You'd think that your brain would be on your side in a long-distance race," Dad said. "But it isn't. Your brain is your worst enemy when you run long distances. Your brain is on your body's side, and believe me, after your body has spent eighteen hours running up and down mountains, it just wants to go home, lie down on the couch and inhale a bag of barbecue chips."

He squirted water into his baseball cap and put it back on his head. Streams of water dribbled down the back of his neck.

"Oh sure," he went on, "every now and again, your brain will play nice. It'll say something optimistic like: 'The bath you take after this race sure is going to feel good!' Or, 'It sure is great, being outside in the fresh air!' But most of the time your brain just lobs grenades at you. Things like, 'You're stupid for trying this; you should drop out and go home.' Or: 'NO WAY can you run a hundred miles! What are you, crazy?'"

It began to drizzle. The mist was whiter than snow. I had no idea how close we were to the top of the mountain.

"But always remember," Dad said, "the trail demons aren't real. It's just your mind, trying to get you to stop. Don't fall for it. Don't let anything stop you. Nothing is impossible. You'll be amazed what you're capable of."

We climbed for another hour, and then, quite suddenly, we popped through the roof of the cloud. The sun shone down and heated our faces, and steam rose off of our arms and legs. Chimney Top's flat peak was straight ahead. It looked as though someone had sliced the top off the mountain with a bread knife.

"Don't lean forward so much," Dad told me. "Just imagine there's a huge magnet at the top of the mountain and you've got a band of steel wrapped around your chest. Imagine that the magnet is pulling you up the hill. There you go. We're almost there. Keep going!"

Eventually we reached the summit and stared down at an ocean of grey. Red-tailed hawks flew in circles, and between the breaks in the cloud, I could see the long silver finger of Hither Lake.

Dad opened a bag of trail mix and a carton of chocolate milk, and we ate and drank and didn't say much.

"This is a beautiful place where we live," Dad said at last. "Of all the places I've been, this is the nicest."

He used that word, *nicest*, but I knew he was thinking *safest*. Dad liked Canada because it's safe. He was always talking about that.

"You're so serious," he said, turning to me. "What are you thinking about?"

I looked up at him and smiled. "I'm thinking . . . I just climbed a mountain!"

BEWARE THE CHAIR
Mile 22

SYDNEY WATSON WALTERS: That surprised you? That you climbed up the mountain?

QUINN: Totally. It was the first time I did something that I thought was impossible. It was the first time I really felt proud of myself.

SYDNEY WATSON WALTERS: Most of us only dream about doing the impossible. But you've actually gone and done it. What was the best thing about the 100-mile race?

QUINN: The food.

SYDNEY WATSON WALTERS: The food? Seriously?

QUINN: For sure! I don't know if you know this, but long-distance running is probably the only sport in the world where the athletes get to eat piles and piles of CRAP. Well, aside from bowling, anyway. Ever watch bowling on TV? Those people aren't eating salads.

Anyway, here are the foods I normally eat in my real life:

Salmon and trout
Chicken
Brown bread
Broccoli and kale
Corn
Asparagus
Bean salad
Water
MILK!
Almond butter
Low-fat yogurt
Beets and yams
Lentil soup

Disgustingly healthy stuff, I'm sure you'll agree. My mom's into healthy eating, what can I say? Now, check out what they feed you at 100-mile races:

Chocolate-chip cookies
Salt-and-vinegar chips
Baked potatoes
Pretzels
Hamburgers and burritos
Candy bars
Root beer, ginger ale, cream soda
Chocolate- and yogurt-covered raisins
Pizza

SYDNEY WATSON WALTERS: Why so much junk food?

QUINN: When you run 100 miles, you need LOTS of energy. And the fastest way to get energy is from fatty foods and sugar. Salt's important too, since it keeps your muscles from cramping up. That's why they feed you potato chips and pretzels.

Anyway, when I got to Silver Valley, there was all this awesome food spread out on a table. Unfortunately, my stomach was feeling pukey, so I didn't feel at all like eating.

SYDNEY WATSON WALTERS: You keep talking about these rest stops. Can you describe what Silver Valley looked like?

QUINN: It was like a movie set in the middle of the forest. Music was pounding, and little kids were running in and out of tents. But the thing I remember best are the volunteers. They were amazing. They cheered as I jogged into the clearing, as if I'd won Olympic gold. That bald guy in the kilt was flipping burgers over a firepit.

"Hey there, Lucky Number Thirteen!" Bruce shouted. "What can I get you?"

I looked at the burgers sizzling on the grill. They were shiny with grease. "Nothing right now," I said.

Bruce cracked open a can of cherry-flavoured Perk. "Don't tell me," he said, "you're a vegetarian, right?"

He took a sip of his drink and slid a tray of baked yams across the table. The ropes in my stomach tightened. "Pass," I said.

"Ya gotta eat something," Bruce said. "You've got seventy-eight miles left to go."

I shook my head. "No thanks," I said. I walked over to a camp chair set up beside the clearing.

"Don't sit in that," said Bruce.

I looked up. "Why not?" I said.

"Beware the chair," Bruce said.

Beware the chair?

"If you sit down, your muscles will tighten up," he said. "You might not get up again. It's happened to a lot of runners over the years."

I stared at him for a moment, trying to figure out if he was serious. He was, so I walked over to the picnic table.

I refilled my water bottle and my hydration pack — a mix of half water, half sports drink. I took a long drink and reholstered my bottle, then looked around for Kneecap and Ollie. The hatchback wasn't in the parking lot, so I figured they were still on the road. I walked back to the food table.

There were bowls full of peanuts and jelly beans, and plates filled with those weird cookies with the red jam in the middle. Who eats those? I wondered.

Bruce put his spatula down and walked over. "How much have you had to drink?" he asked.

"Lots," I said.

"Mmm." He picked up my hands and inspected my palms. He pressed each of my fingers and then he did the same thing with my wrists. "Any stomach problems?" he asked.

"No," I lied.

He let go of my hands. "What colour is your pee?" he asked.

He might as well have been asking about the weather.

"I'm not sure," I stammered.

"Keep an eye on it," Bruce said. "You want it to be clear. If it's dark yellow or brown, you need to drink more water."

I nodded and looked up at Chimney Top. A thin white line — a river — was carrying fresh rainwater down from the top.

"Follow me," Bruce said suddenly.

He led me to the side of the medical tent and made me stand on a scale. The digital read-out blinked for a second, and then a number popped up: 106. "You're down a pound from when you started," he said, squinting at his clipboard. "That's not bad, but you need to keep drinking. We've got water, apple juice, Perk and ginger ale. Which do you want?"

"Perk please," I said.

Bruce shook his head. "Try some ginger ale."

He slopped some into a paper cup.

"Could you stir the bubbles out of it?" I asked.

"Sure."

He stirred it with a spoon and handed me the cup. He watched as I drank it, stroking his sideburns with his fingers. "I'm sorry that your dad isn't running this one," he said. "We always had a good time when he was around."

Bruce looked at me expectantly, but I didn't know what to say. I didn't feel like talking about my father.

Something exploded in the trees behind us. It was as loud as fireworks. A brown ball of feathers skittered this way and that.

My heart raced. Bruce burst out laughing. "It's only a wild turkey," he said. "Right there, see?"

He pointed at the bird, which had come to a sudden stop a few metres away. It was grey and black, and nearly invisible against the dead leaves on the forest floor. It was three times as big as a pigeon.

"Those stupid birds don't budge until you're right on top of them," Bruce said. "Then they make all that racket. Gives me a heart attack every time."

Someone shouted from the far side of the clearing.

"QUINN? NO WAY! Hey there, Q-Tip!"

Kneecap rushed over and gave me a hug. Instantly, she sprang back. "Yuck!" she cried. "You're slimy!"

"Sorry," I said.

She grinned. "Jeez you're fast," she said. "How long have you been here?"

"About five minutes," I said. "Where are Ollie and Mom?"

"They spun down to a bakery in Torrance. We weren't expecting you for another hour."

"But I told you I'd be here by ten," I said.

"I know," said Kneecap. "But we didn't believe you."

I didn't know whether to be pleased by this or not.

Kneecap looked me up and down. "You're looking strong, tiger," she said. "What place is he in, Bruce?"

Bruce ran a finger down his clipboard. "Quinn Scheurmann, let's see . . . " He flipped back a page. "Actually, he's sixth."

Me? Quinn Scheurmann? In sixth place?

Bruce held the clipboard out so I could see. He'd been placing check marks beside the names of the runners as they passed through the rest stop. So far there weren't very many marks.

"That's got to be wrong," I said. "I can't be in sixth."

"Why not?" said Bruce.

"Because I'm a kid," I said. "And my legs are shorter than everyone else's."

A burst of applause erupted behind us, and another runner staggered into the camp. The new arrival raised his fist in the air and then promptly lay down on the ground.

"Check out those socks," Kneecap whispered. "Hoo boy, that is some stylin' toe-wear!"

It was the creep who'd told me to drop out of the race.

Bruce walked over to meet the new arrival. I watched him offer Mr. Dirt Eater a burger.

Kneecap peeled a banana. She was wearing her Raptors T-shirt and a pair of puke-green flip-flops.

"Thanks for inviting me out here," she said. "It's good to be hanging out with you again."

I picked up a rope of red licorice and took a bite. Of all the food I could see, it was the only thing that appealed.

"How long do you think it's been?" Kneecap asked. "I mean, this is the first time you and I have hung out in months."

I chewed the licorice for a long time before swallowing. It went down okay. I took another bite.

"You know I got suspended, right?" she said.

Mom told me you should chew each mouthful sixty times. Chew, chew, chew. Kneecap was staring at me.

"You didn't call," she went on. "I thought you would, but you didn't."

"I meant to," I said. Chew, chew, chew.

"Yeah, but you didn't."

A metal flavour filled my mouth. It tasted like I was sucking on a penny.

"You know," said Kneecap, "those doctors say you have a big heart. But you never use it for anything but running."

A muscle in my right leg started twitching. There were tears in Kneecap's eyes. She was close to crying.

"I invited you to come to this race," I muttered.

"I know," said Kneecap. "And I'm glad you did. But seriously, Quinn, you can't keep icing me out. Not if you want us to stay friends."

That hit me like a punch in the stomach.

Kneecap wiped her eyes with the sleeve of her shirt. "Anyway," she said, "I'm glad you're running this race. I know you've had a cruddy year and everything. But it's about time you cleaned yourself up."

I looked away. People shouldn't tell people to clean themselves up. It's a mean thing to say, even if it's true.

"Oh, come on," said Kneecap. "Don't get mad at me again. You know exactly what I'm talking about."

I didn't answer. The ropes in my stomach were knotting up.

"If you want to hang on to your friends," Kneecap said, "you can't hide in your bedroom and not talk to anyone. How many of your friends have stuck by you this year? Just one. Me. And sometimes I'm not sure why."

A tornado was swimming up my throat. It was coming out. Sweat poured down my face.

I dashed into the woods.

"Quinn, what's wrong? Quinn? QUINN?"

There wasn't much food in my stomach to throw up. Licorice, ginger ale, a couple of litres of water. On the bright side, I got a good abdominal workout.

"You all right?" Kneecap shouted.

"Yeah," I managed to choke out.

I rinsed my mouth with a squirt of water. Then I walked back to the picnic table and stood close to Kneecap.

"Toss your cookies?" she asked.

"Yeah." I hung my head between my knees. It took me a minute to get my breath back.

"Sit down," she said.

"I can't," I said.

"Why not?"

"Because I might not get up again."

Kneecap rolled her eyes.

"Seriously," I said. "Bruce told me to beware the chair."

"This isn't a chair," Kneecap said, "it's a picnic table." She yanked me down onto the bench beside her.

"Feeling better?"

"A bit." It felt nice to sit down. Really nice. Amazingly, I was feeling a bit hungry. I grabbed a handful of potato chips. I wanted salt. "Did Bruce see me puke?" I asked.

Kneecap looked over at the firepit. "No, he's been talking to the old guy in the socks," she said.

The Dirt Eater was standing on the scale, holding on to Bruce for support.

"He doesn't look too good," said Kneecap. "A hundred bucks says he won't finish the race."

"He probably won't leave this rest stop," I said.

A bead of sweat dripped off my forehead and landed on the wooden seat between my legs. I reached down and traced a figure eight in the tiny puddle. It dried almost instantly in the sun.

"Uh, Quinn . . . I'm sorry I said all that stuff," said Kneecap. "Not exactly good timing, is it?"

I didn't say anything.

"I only brought it up because I miss you, you know?"

For a while we didn't say anything to each other. A purple

butterfly fluttered around us and then landed on the middle knuckle of Kneecap's right hand. I watched as it stretched out its wings.

"I better get going," I said finally.

"But you just threw up."

"I feel fine," I said. "Everyone throws up in these races."

I stood up. For a moment, the world went black, and tiny white comets flared past my eyes. When the world reappeared, I stumbled across the parking lot and made my way over to Bruce. The Dirt Eater was sitting in a camp chair, staring down the hill toward the lake.

"Seriously, didn't you see it?" he was saying.

Bruce shook his head. "No. I didn't."

"What about you?" Dirt Eater said, turning to face me. "Did you see it?"

"See what?" I said.

"The school bus," he said. "It just drove across the lake."

I looked out at the lake. It was robin's-egg blue.

"I don't see anything," I said.

"Wow!" the man shouted. "There it goes again!"

Bruce and I squinted at the lake. I saw whitecaps, green hills, but — surprise surprise — no school bus.

"Why don't you lie down for a while, Ted," Bruce said.

Dirt Eater scowled. "I don't need to lie down," he said.

Bruce shook his head. "Just for a while," he said. "Just until we can get your blood sugar up a little bit."

The Dirt Eater glared at Bruce, then threw his water bottle down the hill. "It's this kid you ought to bench," he muttered. "He's way too young to be running this race."

I said nothing. I hate it when people tell me I'm too

young. Wayne Gretzky scored 300 goals when he was eleven. Annaleise Carr swam across Lake Ontario when she was fourteen. No one told *them* they were too young.

"Take it easy, Ted," said Bruce. "This young boy is Tom Scheurmann's son. He knows a thing or two about running."

Dirt Eater grumbled and turned back to the lake.

Bruce leaned over to me. "Don't worry about him," he whispered. "He's just going through a bad spell. Hallucinations."

The trail demons, I thought. Dad told me they always turned up after 35 miles. We'd only run 22 so far. I guess Mr. Dirt Eater was in for a long day.

Just then, a silver hatchback pulled into the parking lot. The doors popped open and Mom and Ollie sprang out.

Mom was wearing a yellow sundress tied with a green cord. Ollie was holding a cardboard box. "It's Speedy Quinnzales!" he shouted.

Mom walked over and gave me a hug. "How are you feeling?" she asked.

"Pretty good," I said.

"You've got colour in your cheeks," she said. "Are you wearing sunscreen?"

"SPF 70," I said.

"Good." She turned to Bruce. "Has he been eating?"

Bruce shrugged. "I weighed him and he looks okay."

Mom lifted the lid of the cardboard box. A dozen Nanaimo bars glistened in the sunshine. "What do you say to these?" she asked.

Nanaimo bars are usually my favourite. But not today. My stomach lurched.

"I'm not really hungry," I said.

This threw Mom into high alert. She pressed her palm to my forehead. "What day is your birthday?" she asked.

"Mom," I said, "I'm fine. Really."

She wasn't buying it. She was twirling her magic lasso of truth. "What day is your birthday?" she repeated.

"August third," I sighed.

"And where do you live?"

"135 Champlain Drive."

Ollie grabbed a Nanaimo bar and folded it into his mouth. Mom was too busy asking me skill-testing questions to notice. What was the name of my first-grade teacher? My favourite colour? My Pinterest login?

Ollie gulped down the Nanaimo bar and interrupted. "You've got a suntan on your legs," he said.

I looked down. "That's not a tan, that's dirt," I said. I tried to scrape off the layer of crud but it stuck to me like sap.

"Did you visit the Shrine yet?" Ollie asked.

"Not yet," I said. "It's still seventy-five miles away."

"Oh."

He reached for another Nanaimo bar, but Mom zapped him with her laser-beam eyes. Reluctantly, he withdrew his hand.

"It's only ten-thirty," Mom said, turning back to me. "You got here too quickly. You promised you'd take it easy, remember?"

"I *am* taking it easy," I said.

"Not easy enough. You know what your father would say. Take it slow. Enjoy the scenery. Smell the flowers."

I seriously doubted that my father would tell me to smell the flowers. More likely he'd just say, "Be the tortoise, not the hare."

Bruce topped up my water bottle one last time and handed me a plastic bag full of salted yams. "Eat as many of these as you can," he told me. He looked me in the eye and spoke real quietly. "Seriously," he said, "eat as many as you can."

"What are they?" Ollie asked, squinching up his face.

"Sweet potatoes," I said.

"Rocket fuel," Bruce corrected.

I squeezed the bag into my fanny pack. "Time for me to get going," I said.

Mom's smile sagged. It looked like a laundry line in December. "But we only just got here," she said.

"Now now," said Bruce. "This isn't a social visit. The kid's running a race. And he's right, he's got to go."

Mom knelt down to double-knot my shoelaces. "Are you sure you've had enough to eat?" she asked.

"Yes," I sighed.

"He shouldn't even be running," the Dirt Eater growled. "He's way too young to be running this kind of distance."

"That's enough, Ted," Bruce said.

Mom glanced over at the Dirt Eater.

"See you later!" I shouted.

"Wait!" said Ollie. "Don't you want a joke?"

I smiled at my brother. "Definitely," I said.

Ollie grinned. "Knock knock," he said.

"Who's there?" I said.

"Lettuce."

"Lettuce who?"

"Lettuce in, it's freezing cold out here!"

The adults all laughed, except for the Dirt Eater. He was still preoccupied with his imaginary school bus on the lake.

Mom gave me a hug. "Make lots of noise out there," she said. "Let those bears know you're coming."

"Sure thing," I said.

"Promise me you'll sing," she said. "You used to sing all the time. Why don't you sing anymore?"

I tried to swallow, but my spit had dried up. "Probably something to do with puberty," I said.

CHIMNEY TOP
Mile 23

I was happy to get going. The longer I hung around, smelling those burgers, the more I wanted to lie down and take a nap. Those camp chairs looked comfy! And my legs were already starting to ache.

In case you're wondering, I had 78 miles to go. Which is roughly the distance between your house and, oh, I don't know, the *moon*.

That's how far I still needed to run before dawn. And I only had 19 hours and 12 minutes left to do it.

Just as I started jogging down the trail, Kneecap came running up behind me. "Wait up, Q-Tip!" she shouted.

She sprinted over. She'd changed out of her flip-flops and was wearing proper trail shoes.

"What's up?" I said.

"Peace offering," she said. She held out her hand. A small plastic chip sat in her palm.

"What's that?" I asked.

"Extra battery," she said. "For the phone. You'll need it — that thing is an energy hog."

I took the battery and slipped it into my fanny pack. "Thanks," I said.

"Don't make too many calls," she said. "The roaming charges are brutal. But you can text for free."

I tugged the zipper shut and snapped the belt tight around my waist. "Thanks," I said.

Kneecap grinned. "I have another surprise."

"What?" I said.

"I'm running with you."

SYDNEY WATSON WALTERS: Seriously? Is Kneecap an athlete?

QUINN: She's super skinny, but she's about as athletic as a door-stop. The only exercise she likes is running off her mouth.

(Audience laughs)

SYDNEY WATSON WALTERS: Are friends allowed to run on the racecourse?

QUINN: It's a very casual race, so people can do what they want. It's not like it's the Boston Marathon or anything. Still, I wasn't too thrilled about having her along.

"You know I'm going up that mountain, right?" I said. I pointed up at Chimney Top.

"That little thing?" Kneecap said. She shrugged her shoulders.

I shook my head. The truth was, I didn't want her to slow me down. But I couldn't tell her that, not after she'd given me the battery.

"Don't look so worried," Kneecap said. "I'll only come a few miles."

Her shoes were brand new. It suddenly hit me: she'd bought them especially for today, so she could run with me!

"Most people don't just decide to climb a mountain," I said. "Usually they do some training first."

Kneecap glared at me. "I'm not doing this because I want to," she snapped. "I'm doing it because I'm trying to be your *friend*!"

With that, she jogged ahead of me up the road. I walked behind her, feeling like a chump.

"You do know that I've been running since dawn, right?" I called out. "My sparkling personality might have fizzled a bit."

"Ya think?" she shouted back. She jogged even faster.

I thought: When will this race start being fun?

The pink trail flags turned right, leading us onto a trail rutted with tread marks. The path ran uphill, alongside a chain of foamy pools and waterfalls. The smell of rotting wood filled the forest, and the gurgling stream sounded like babies laughing. The trail became steeper and zigzagged back and forth in sharp switchbacks. It felt like we were climbing stairs.

I watched the backs of Kneecap's brown legs as we jogged. I could tell that she was starting to hurt. Sure enough, pretty soon she slowed down and started walking. I ran up beside her.

"How can you do this?" she gasped.

"Do what?" I said.

"Run a hundred miles like this? It's insane."

The corners of her mouth were turned down.

"I have superpowers, remember?"

"Oh, right," she said. "I forgot."

We spent the next 15 minutes climbing what my dad had called the apron of the mountain. Only this time there wasn't any mist, so we could see how high we were getting. When we came to a clearing, I saw a tiny boat crossing Hither Lake, half a kilometre below. Little black waves fanned out behind it like a capital V. I stopped while Kneecap gasped for breath. "You're not even breathing hard," she said, looking at me. "We really need to get you a spandex costume."

She was being sarcastic, but I figured I'd play along. "I need a superhero name first," I said.

"How about Puke Man?" Kneecap suggested.

Ha. Funny. Play it cool, I thought. "Doesn't really have a great ring to it," I said.

"I guess not," agreed Kneecap. "How about Skeletor?"

"I'm not that skinny," I said.

"Sure you are. You've got legs like a chicken."

"Do not," I said.

"Do too," said Kneecap. "They're kinda cute though."

We continued climbing. Kneecap said, "Forget about the name. What you need is a good catchphrase."

"Like how the Hulk says, 'It's clobbering time!'"

"Yeah, but that one's already taken," said Kneecap.

I thought for a moment. "What about: Best Foot Forward?"

Kneecap shrieked with laughter. "That's the lamest thing I ever heard!"

I laughed too. It *was* pretty lame, I had to admit. "How about Run Like Snot!" I offered.

"Not bad," said Kneecap. "How about To The Finish Line And Beyond!"

"Meh," I said.

"Wait a second," said Kneecap. "I've got it. Kick Some Shins!"

Her face was bright red, so I suggested we take a break. We stepped back from the cliff face and sat down in the shade.

"Seriously," she said. "Kick Some Shins. That's pretty good, right?"

"Good-ish," I said.

Kneecap glanced at the forest behind us. "Aren't you worried about the bears?" she asked.

"Not yet," I said. "But ask me again tonight, when it gets dark."

She crawled back to the ledge and looked down at the valley. She shivered. "Have you been singing much?" she asked.

"A bit," I said.

"Don't tell me," she said. "'Run Baby Run'?"

"I've written other songs besides that one," I said.

She smiled. "I know. I'm just teasing."

Just then, I heard a familiar noise. Jingle bells. I swung around.

"Hey there, Lucky Number Thirteen!"

Kara was bounding up the trail behind us.

"I thought you were *ahead* of me," I said.

"I was," Kara laughed. "Until my body fell apart, that is.

I spent a half hour cooling my legs in the lake."

Her knee was wrapped in a tensor bandage.

"What happened?" I asked.

"It's nothing," she said. "The cold water brought down the swelling a bit, plus I've got lots of Advil." She turned to Kneecap and threw out her hand. "Hi there," she said. "I'm Kara."

"This is my friend Kneecap," I said.

They shook hands. "Pleased to meet you," said Kara. "Did you lose your number, or are you a bandit?"

"What's a bandit?" said Kneecap.

"Someone who runs the race illegally."

Kneecap thought about this. "I'm not running the race," she said. "I'm just here for moral support."

"Sort of," I said.

Kneecap glared at me.

A red squirrel scolded us from the top of a tree. Kara stepped around the two of us and continued bounding up the hill. "Come on!" she called back. "Let's make some time!"

We did our best to keep up with her. "Kara's a cop," I explained to Kneecap.

"Really?" Kneecap said. "And here we are, breaking the speed limit!"

The path veered right and we crossed a huge basin filled with loose scree. Kara led the way, hopping from boulder to boulder.

"How much farther to the top?" Kneecap asked.

"Probably about a mile," said Kara.

The trail edged back to the cliff, and the three of us found ourselves walking in single file along a narrow ledge.

A curl of blue smoke rose out of the valley far below. Kara scrabbled along the path like a mountain goat.

"The wind's strong up here," I said.

"Cold too," said Kneecap.

"Enjoy it while you can," said Kara. "It'll be hotter than an oven on the other side."

I looked back at Kneecap. Her face was greenish grey, the colour of pressure-treated wood.

"You okay?" I called out.

She was staring at the water far below. "This is the craziest sport in the world," she said.

We walked a little farther and the trail broadened out. Relieved, I moved back from the ledge. Kara stood at the top of the ridge, waiting for us to catch up. Kneecap bent over and rubbed the backs of her legs. "What do they give you when you cross the finish line?" she asked. "A car?"

"A belt buckle," Kara said.

Kneecap's smile folded. "A *what*?" she said.

"Belt buckle."

Kneecap shot me a you-gotta-be-joking look.

"And get this," Kara added. "You only get the belt buckle if you finish in twenty-four hours. Take longer than that and you don't get anything at all."

Kneecap shook her head in disbelief. "Nuts, nuts, totally nuts," she said.

"Kara won this race last year," I said.

"No *way*."

"Way."

Kneecap smiled weakly at Kara. "And all you got for it was a belt buckle?" she said.

"It's not about the prize," said Kara.

"What's it about?"

"Enduring."

A gust of wind threw us against the rock face. We crouched down. Kneecap was still massaging her legs.

"You okay, hon?" Kara asked.

"I think I've got shin splints."

"Those aren't your shins."

"Really? What are they?"

"Your calves."

Kneecap smirked. "Yeah? So I've got calf splints then."

The sunlight flickered, and I glanced up. A glider plane, white as a ghost, circled silently above our heads. Chimney Top's blunted summit loomed not far away. We still had to get to the top of that crest.

"Come on," said Kara. "Final push."

Ten minutes later we reached the summit. The wind was fierce, so we walked in single file across the plateau. Kara went first, then me, then Kneecap. At last we came to the massive blade of rock that everyone calls the Shark's Fin. We sat down behind it, sheltered from the wind. Kara shrugged off her hydration pack and leaned back against the rock.

"Anyone want raisins?" she asked.

Kneecap took a handful. Her face was blotchy and her shirt was soaked with sweat.

"Having fun?" Kara asked her.

"No," said Kneecap. "It feels like my brain has turned to oatmeal."

"Want some yams?" I asked, pulling out my bag.

"Have they got salt on them? Yessss!"

Kneecap popped a chunk of sweet potato into her mouth and closed her eyes.

"That'll give you strength," Kara said.

"It tastes like I'm eating the sun," said Kneecap.

I stared down at the valley. It was misty green, and hay-coloured sunshine fell in stripes over the hills. I unclasped my hydration pack and pulled out the bladder to see how much water I had left. I'd drunk a lot on the trip up the mountain, but the bladder was still three-quarters full. I stuffed it back into the hydration pack.

"How did you get your nickname?" Kara asked Kneecap.

"My older brother gave it to me," Kneecap said, swinging her legs back and forth.

"She used to knee him," I said. "Where it counts."

Kara winced. "There are laws against that," she said.

"I was just a kid," said Kneecap.

For a few moments, nobody said anything. Kara and Kneecap chewed their raisins.

"Speaking of nicknames," Kneecap said, turning to me, "I figured out your superhero name."

"What is it?" I said.

She smiled at me. "The Lactator."

"The what?" I said.

"Isn't that one of your superpowers?" she asked. "Your body makes a ton of lactic acid, right?"

"No," I said. "It doesn't make much."

"Oh," said Kneecap. "Then it's not such a good name."

Kara repacked her bag of raisins. "I haven't got a clue what you kids are talking about," she said.

"Wait a second," said Kneecap. "What about Ultra Boy?

You're a boy, and you run ultra-marathons."

"This is the first one I've run," I said. "And I haven't even finished it yet."

"Details, details," said Kneecap. "I think Ultra Boy rocks."

I looked down the mountain. A line of colourful dots was bobbing up the trail we'd just climbed. Other runners.

"Break time's over," said Kara. "Ready to push on?"

"No thanks," said Kneecap. "My work here is done. You two will have to carry on without me."

I almost felt an ache, hearing those words. "You could come with us to the next rest stop," I said.

"How far is that?" asked Kneecap.

"Seventeen miles."

Kneecap laughed. "I've had enough exercise for one day," she said. "Actually, I've had enough for the whole year!"

Kara slung her hydration pack over her shoulders. "Nice meeting you, Kneecap," she said.

"Ditto," said Kneecap.

The two of them high-fived. Kneecap gave me a military salute. I saluted back, and then she turned and walked away.

"Be careful on the ledges," I shouted.

"Yeah, yeah," she replied.

When she rounded the edge of Shark's Fin, the wind blew her hair straight back and her face turned golden brown in the sunshine. Then she dropped out of sight and was gone.

"Cool kid," said Kara. "Not much of a runner though."

"Come on," I said. "We're losing time."

A DIFFERENT KIND
OF SPORT

SYDNEY WATSON WALTERS: How long have you and Kneecap been friends?

QUINN: Ever since she moved to our neighbourhood. We're in the same year at school and we used to sit together on the bus. And of course, we started the UHL together.

SYDNEY WATSON WALTERS: The UHL?

QUINN: Last year at school, Kneecap made this amazing discovery. She kicked a quarter across the floor of the boys' washroom, and it ricocheted off the rounded lip where the floor meets the wall and flew into the air. Somehow she got the angle just right and the quarter landed right in the urinal! It was a perfect goal. And that's how urinal hockey was born.

SYDNEY WATSON WALTERS: So UHL stands for . . .

QUINN: The Urinal Hockey League. We had eight teams — The Whiz Kids, The Main Vein Drainers, The Double Flushers . . . We even had an anthem for the league.

SYDNEY WATSON WALTERS: Someone wrote a song about urinal hockey?

QUINN: I did! We used to sing it before all the games. It goes to the tune of "God Save the Queen."

> *God save our humble can,*
> *Smelly and pee–stained can,*
> *God save our can!*
> *Lead us victorious,*
> *Yellow and glorious,*
> *Please don't flatulate over us,*
> *God save our can!*

SYDNEY WATSON WALTERS: That's very . . . creative!

QUINN: We had twenty games in the regular season, then the playoffs after that. We played two on two, with 5-minute periods. Whenever someone scored, the losing goalie would have to pick the quarter out of the urinal with his fingers.

SYDNEY WATSON WALTERS: Sounds . . . um . . . disgusting.

QUINN: Everyone washed their hands right after. I also invented the "fresh flush" rule.

SYDNEY WATSON WALTERS: And Kneecap was involved in this? Even though the games were played in the boys' washroom?

QUINN: Kneecap never had any problem with that. None of the boys minded either, since she was one of our best players.

The trouble began when Kneecap started bringing other girls into the league. I'm all for equality, but it wasn't smart, sneaking ten girls into the boys' washroom every lunch hour.

SYDNEY WATSON WALTERS: The teachers caught on, I gather?

QUINN: Yeah. Kneecap got suspended for a week. I thought I was going to get nailed too, but I didn't.

SYDNEY WATSON WALTERS: Why not? Did Kneecap protect you?

QUINN: She must have. She's pretty loyal.

SYDNEY WATSON WALTERS: I've got a crazy question for you, Quinn Scheurmann.

QUINN: What?

SYDNEY WATSON WALTERS: Remember how Kneecap called you a fun vampire? I'm curious . . . When's the last time you had some fun?

QUINN: I don't know. Maybe at last year's Hallowe'en dance? Actually, no. That wasn't fun at all.

I didn't see Kneecap until the end of the night. I don't like dancing very much, especially when I'm wearing a lame Hallowe'en costume, so I spent most of the evening in the cafeteria, playing cards.

At eight-thirty I wandered down to the gym. Kneecap ran over from her group of friends and grabbed my hand.

"Where have you been hiding?" she asked.

"Nowhere," I said.

Her body was encased in a bunch of cardboard cubes. She'd painted them red, green, blue and yellow. Her head poked out of a yellow cube on top.

"What *are* you?" I asked.

"A game of Tetris, dummy!" she said.

She looked like a giant letter L, perched on two skinny legs wrapped in black leggings. She was wearing red Converse sneakers with Tetris-themed shoelaces. It looked like she'd painted the Tetris shapes herself.

"What are you?" she asked me. "A doctor?"

"A *killer* doctor," I said, showing off the fake blood on my hands.

Kneecap nodded, unimpressed. "Didn't you wear those scrubs last year?"

"That was two years ago," I said. "I was a marathon runner last year."

"Of course. How could I forget?" Kneecap put her hands on her hips, which were a metre wide with all those cubes. She was wearing a little bit of makeup, I noticed, which she didn't usually do.

"Come on," she said, pulling me toward the dance floor. Her hand felt soft, like the grips on my handlebars. Her friends were watching us from the corner of the gym.

"You can actually dance in that costume?" I said.

"Of course! I've been dancing all night."

To prove this, she did a little twirl and accidentally hit a grade-seven boy dressed as Thor.

"Sorry, Thor!" Kneecap said.

"He's the Hammer God, he can take it," I said.

Kneecap kept dancing. "Come on, Q-Tip! Show me what you've got!"

"I'm not a very good dancer," I said.

"Who cares?" she said. "This isn't *Dancing With the Stars*."

"But I don't really like this song," I muttered.

"You don't like any normal songs," Kneecap said.

"Sure I do," I said. "I like Bovine Ancestry. And Trout-spawn."

"Oh, come on," said Kneecap. "A vacuum cleaner makes better music than those guys. And it's impossible to dance to that stuff."

Just then, the song "Don't Stop Believin'" came on.

"Perfect!" Kneecap squealed. "You *have* to dance to this one!"

Everyone was swarming onto the dance floor.

"But it's lame," I said. "You know that it's lame."

"You're lame," Kneecap said. "Come on, it's late, and we *need* to dance."

She dragged me to the centre of the gym while strobe lights flashed atop the stacks of speakers. She surprised me by putting her arms around my neck, even though everyone else was doing their best air guitar. I put my hands on either side of Kneecap's cubes, and we staggered back and forth in a weird boxy shuffle. Kneecap smelled nice, like green-apple jelly beans. I was nervous, and left sweaty handprints all over her cardboard.

"You okay?" she asked.

"Yeah," I said. "But it's a little bit awkward."

She detached the cubes around her shoulders and arms. She also took the yellow box away from her head. "That better?" she said.

It wasn't really, since she still had cubes around her waist. Kneecap smushed her cheek against my neck. "This is nice," she said. "I've wanted to do this for a while."

Off to our right, thirty kids swayed back and forth in a big circle. Zombies, soldiers, sexy cats. A group of grade-seven boys grinned at me from the stage. My friend Spencer was up there, laughing.

"Hey, Quinn!" he shouted. "Your girlfriend's a square!"

I glared at him. What's your deal? I thought.

"Something wrong?" Kneecap whispered in my ear.

"No," I said.

But something was. I had a gross feeling in my stomach, as if I'd drunk too much pop. But I also felt happy to be dancing with Kneecap.

"Careful!" Spencer shouted. "She's got a wide load!"

I shot Spencer my death stare. You snot rocket, I mouthed.

Kneecap didn't seem to notice any of this, but I felt really embarrassed for some reason. So I did something really dumb. I took Kneecap's hand from the back of my neck and stuck it straight out, like the spout of a watering can. Then I swayed Kneecap back and forth, with our hands stuck straight out, like we were a waltzing teapot or something.

"What are you doing?" Kneecap said, laughing.

"I'm not sure," I said, tipping her forward. I wanted to get as far away from Spencer as possible.

And then I did something even stupider. The stupidest thing I possibly could have done.

I told a joke. Not just any joke. A *racist* joke.

I'm not sure why I did this, exactly. I only wanted to lighten the mood.

Not surprisingly, Kneecap didn't like the joke very much. She threw away my hand like it was a dirty diaper.

"Why would you tell me *that*?" she asked.

"I was only making conversation!" I sputtered.

"Don't Stop Believin'" came to an end, and the deejay launched an even slower song. The disco ball started spinning. Most of the kids broke off into pairs.

Kneecap stared at me. "Do you even know what a towel-head is?" she said. "Some jerks use it to mean Arabs — people from Saudi Arabia."

I stared at her. I hadn't known that.

"My mom is from Saudi Arabia, you idiot."

She turned and stalked away, stopping to pick up her extra Tetris cubes from the floor. Then she stopped and looked back. "Throw away your weird pills, Quinn," she said.

With that, she walked across the darkened gym, the strobe light flashing off her cardboard outfit. She suddenly looked ridiculous in that costume, and very sad, and I wanted to run over to her and cheer her up, only I couldn't.

For a while after that, she and I didn't talk very much. Actually, we didn't talk at all. Kneecap never sat beside me in Science class anymore. And I didn't sit with her on the bus, since I was running to and from school every day.

For a day or two, I was confused about what had happened. But then I thought about what I'd said. That towel-head joke. What a boneheaded thing to say.

But here's the weird part: It was my dad who told me that joke. Did that make him a racist? Was *I* a racist for repeating it?

I decided that I needed to ask my dad about it. I'd do it on Sunday, the next time he Skyped. But that was the first Sunday that Dad didn't call. And so the towel-head thing got swept under the carpet.

THE BONK
Mile 29

With Kneecap gone, Kara exploded down the path, plunging left and right down a chute of sun-baked stones. A third of the way down the mountain, we skirted a giant bowl of rock and scrabbled over boulders as large as couches. I felt totally out of control, charging downhill at death-defying angles, my legs running faster than the rest of my body could keep up. Kara, as usual, was incredibly fast. Gravity didn't seem to apply to her.

We dropped below the treeline and ran through a forest of evergreens. They were tall and pressed closely together, and the branches felt like razor blades as they brushed against my arms and neck. It was hot again and sweat poured off my skin. I felt like I'd been dunked in cooking oil.

Three-quarters of an hour later we reached the foot of the mountain. We stopped for a break in a meadow filled with purple wildflowers. My legs felt like rubber, and my brain was mush. I turned around and looked at the mountain behind us.

"Did we really just climb over that?" I said.

Chimney Top shimmered in the haze. Kara nodded.

Clouds dotted the sky.

"Think it's going to storm tonight?" I asked.

"Hard to say. Maybe."

We walked along the trail. A flat, grassy swamp stretched out ahead of us. Wooden duckboards had been laid across the marsh, but many of the planks had broken, or rotted away. As we walked, dozens of tiny frogs leapt from the mud banks, barking out froggy yelps as they splashed into the water.

"Look at that one!" Kara said.

The bullfrog was cramming live dragonflies into its mouth. Its jaws were full of wings and eyeballs and legs that were still twitching.

Ollie would love this, I thought to myself. I thought about calling him, but decided against it. Kneecap had said the roaming charges were brutal. So I sent Ollie a text: LOTS OF FROGS OUT HERE.

"We're still behind pace," Kara said, checking her watch. "Come on; let's kick it up a notch."

"Sure thing," I said.

Big mistake!

By now my legs were as weak as rubber bands. I trailed behind, watching Kara's ponytail bounce back and forth.

"It's important to bank lots of miles during the day," Kara shouted. "We'll be a lot slower tonight, after the sun goes down."

She was getting harder and harder to hear. Then, quite suddenly, BLIP — she was a hundred metres ahead. Then,

BLIP — she was a hundred metres farther ahead. My mind was popping in and out like a radio station. BLIP — Kara was a dot on the horizon. BLIP — she was gone.

I stopped, expecting to see her turn around and come back. Then, BLIP — I was lying down on the boardwalk.

When had I decided to take a nap? I didn't remember doing that.

I looked up and noticed a wooden post. There was a sign at the top: Mile 35.

"Things get pretty strange after thirty-five miles," Dad had said. And he was right. Things were definitely getting weird.

Then another BLIP. My shoes had come off. I was wiggling my toes in the sun.

Wait a second! I thought. Who took off my shoes?

I pulled out the bag of sweet potatoes. The wedges were crunchy and loaded with salt. I ate as many as my stomach could handle, then I stuffed the bag back into my pouch.

I took off my hat and dunked it in the swamp. When I put it back on, skunky-smelling water trickled down the back of my neck.

Stand up and start walking, I told myself. If you fall asleep now, you'll never get back up.

Then, BLIP — I was walking. BLIP — the swamp was gone. BLIP — I was back in the forest, and my cap was dry!

I found myself walking down an old logging road. It had deep wheel ruts on both sides, and long grass was growing in between.

Suddenly I heard a noise. Something was humming. Thousands of flies were whining like a chainsaw.

I followed the sound, leaving the trail behind. The smell

of moss and mud filled my nostrils. And something else too — something sweet. I pushed aside some branches and saw a strange sight. Rusty splashes on the ground. Paint? Truck primer?

The sound of the buzzing flies grew louder. Then I saw it. Nastiest thing I've ever seen.

Putrefying flesh, pulsing with white worms. Bloody swatches of brown fur. A pink hoof, covered with ants.

The deer's leg was more than a metre long. No — it was too big to be a deer. Had to be a moose.

What animal was strong enough to tear the leg off a moose?

Coyotes? Wolves?

Something bigger?

Mom's advice came back to me. Don't forget to sing, she'd said.

I suddenly burst into one of my songs. I didn't care if anyone heard; I just wanted to scare the bears away.

> *What he's running from —*
> *To himself he doesn't show.*
> *And what he's running to*
> *Even he doesn't know.*

I slashed my way back to the trail. When I reached it, I started running again. Of course, this little burst of energy didn't last very long. I sprinted for maybe 15 seconds. My heart was pounding like a chopper's rotors.

Then, once again, BLIP — I was lying on the ground. Marshmallow-white clouds were tracking lazily across the sky. I tried to stand up, but I didn't have the strength. I rolled my head sideways and saw a beaver pond.

SYDNEY WATSON WALTERS: Okay, I have to stop you. What the HECK was going on?

QUINN: I was bonking.

SYDNEY WATSON WALTERS: Bonking?

QUINN: I'd run 35 miles, and I hadn't eaten very much. My gas tank was empty. I was all out of go-juice.

SYDNEY WATSON WALTERS: Is bonking the same thing as "hitting the wall"?

QUINN: Yeah. My dad calls it "premature deceleration." It's basically a total brain meltdown.

So there I was, lying on the grass beside this beaver pond. Dead logs stuck out of the water at all angles, with turtles sitting on the logs. Lily pads were everywhere. Water bugs skated across the surface between them. Pinpricks of white light were flashing in my eyes.

That was the good news. The bad news was, the weather was turning to crap. All morning the sky had been as blue as the bottom of a Jacuzzi, or, as my dad would have said, so blue you can smell the paint. But now black clouds were rolling across the sky. They gathered on the horizon like an invading army.

I took off my shoes and shook out two clouds of dirt. A breeze freshened the air and the pond glazed over with ripples.

The clouds got fatter and started climbing into the sky. One was larger than the others. It looked like the head of an octopus.

Whitecaps curled across the pond. Electricity crackled through the air. "Have you seen my shadow?" the octopus cloud said.

SYDNEY WATSON WALTERS: I'm sorry — what happened? You heard a *voice* in the clouds?

QUINN: Yeah. It sounded like sheets snapping on a clothes line. I thought the cloud was talking to me. But it was just a hallucination.

SYDNEY WATSON WALTERS: Which part was the hallucination — the cloud or the voice?

QUINN: The cloud was real, but the voice was something else. It felt like a dream. Only I wasn't sleeping.

The cloud had purple tentacles that reached out over the hills. The tops of the trees thrashed back and forth.

"Have you seen my shadow?" the cloud repeated.

A bird nest glanced off my leg and blew down the trail. My heart was hammering.

"Who wants to know?" I shouted.

The cloud rotated above me. Tree limbs flew through the air like shrapnel.

"Jeez!" I grumbled, pulling my cap down tightly over my head. "Take it easy!"

The cloud changed shape, flattening out like a pie plate. Sand fizzed across bedrock and dirt filled the air.

"Enough with the wind machine!" I cried.

It was in that moment — as I said those five words —

that I realized the voice belonged to the Wind.

Yes, I know. It sounds stupid now. But at the time, I was convinced that I was having a conversation with the Wind. At the same time, I knew it was only a hallucination. I kept hearing my dad's voice saying, "Things get pretty strange after thirty-five miles."

I bent down and dug through my pack for some food and popped a handful of jelly beans into my mouth.

When I looked back up, something had appeared in the sky. It flew toward me like a giant bird, swirling on the updrafts and downdrafts. Eventually it came close enough that I could tell what it was. I reached my hands out and pulled it down to earth.

It was a pair of camouflage pants, size 42 and badly stained. Something was hiding in one of the back pockets.

I pulled it out. It was a folded piece of paper. Someone had written on it. It was my handwriting . . . WAIT!

"Hey!" I shouted. "Where'd you get this?"

Wind said nothing, but the yellow eye glistened. It was a song I'd written the year before.

> The generals who are at the top
> Never get a scratch.
> When soldiers come back, sad and torn
> They send another batch.

It was my anti-war song, "Man Versus Man." I'd written it back in the fall. But then I'd lost it.

"Who'd you steal this from?" I shouted.

Wind didn't answer. I held the waistband of the pants and shook them out. They were pretty disgusting, coated in mud and grime. A roll of Fruity Juicers popped out of the front pocket. I unwrapped the waxed paper and tossed two candies into my mouth. The taste reminded me of afternoons at my house — Dad making toast soldiers for me and Ollie after church. The sound of hot cross buns popping out of the toaster.

Wait a second — how could a candy remind me of all that?

Just a hallucination, I reminded myself.

I crumpled up the wrapper and sat down with my back against a rock. Pillowcases of cloud swirled above the trees.

"Have you seen my shadow?" Wind bellowed.

"Your *shadow*?" I coughed. "You don't *have* a shadow! You're the Wind. You're, like, shadow-free."

Wind blew through the trees, moaning with grief. It sounded like a freight train blowing its horn late at night.

I thought to myself: Why doesn't Wind have a shadow? Everything else has a shadow — doesn't it? Kids have shadows. So do animals. And bicycles. So do cars, mountains, parents.

"Don't worry," I said. "Maybe I'll get lucky and find it. I'm running through the forest anyway, so I'll do some looking."

The octopus cloud lightened to the colour of buttermilk, and spots of blue appeared here and there in the sky.

"Just one question," I shouted. "How will I recognize your shadow if I see it? You're always changing shape. I don't know what you really look like."

But Wind didn't answer. It had already jetted off. It was probably stealing baseball caps from kids in Saskatchewan by now.

I swallowed some of my yams. The sky continued to

brighten. The waves in the beaver pond softened.

What the heck just happened? I wondered.

Some daring frogs began to croak. I stood up, feeling like I was waking from a dream. Then I ate my last sweet-potato wedge and started running.

Thirty-five miles down. Sixty-five to go.

THE BANDIT

Mile 38

Okay, so 100 miles may not sound like such a big deal. But do you know how far it actually is?

It's exactly 160 kilometres. Which is about the distance from Vancouver to Hope. Or from Toronto to London. Or from Montreal to Saint Boniface.

One hundred miles is the distance between:

Edmonton and Red Deer
Calgary and Fort McLeod
Halifax and New Glasgow
Fredericton and Miramichi
Charlottetown and Moncton
Victoria and Port Alberni
Kelowna and Kamloops
Sudbury and Blind River
Hamilton and Owen Sound
Regina and Chaplin
Winnipeg and Carberry
Medicine Hat and Lethbridge

Moose Jaw and Swift Current
Whitehorse and Skagway

I could go on, but basically, if you get in a car, hop on a highway and drive for 2 hours — *that's* 100 miles.

Not many people enter 100-mile races, and of those who do, about half DNF. That's how tough this race is.

SYDNEY WATSON WALTERS: DNF stands for Did Not Finish, right?

QUINN: Yeah. They post it beside your name on the race website after you crash and burn. Most runners I know are embarrassed to get a DNF, but they shouldn't be. There are ten *billion* ways you can implode in this race. You can slip on a wet rock, trip over a tree root, or watch your leg get swallowed by a rabbit hole. If you twist an ankle, like I almost did, congratulations — you just ended your race!

You can eat too much food and wind up with cramps. Or you can eat too little and run out of gas. If you drink too much water, you could even die from a weird condition called hyponatremia. That doesn't happen very often, luckily.

There are other ways to screw up on the trail: You can wear too few clothes and freeze to death. Or you can wear too many and overheat. You can wear the wrong shoes and wind up with blisters. You could wear the wrong kind of shirt, one that chafes against your nipples. Ever had bloody nipples? It hurts like —

SYDNEY WATSON WALTERS: Okay, I get it! It's a really tough race.

QUINN: Exactly. So it's not surprising that I made one tiny mistake.

SYDNEY WATSON WALTERS: What happened?

QUINN: Nothing much. Except . . . Well, it's kind of a miracle that I survived.

SYDNEY WATSON WALTERS: What could be worse than getting bloody nipples?

QUINN: Running out of water.

At first I thought that my back was just sweaty. The sweat trickled down my skin and soaked the waistband of my shorts. But then I noticed that my legs were wet too. Wait a second, I thought. I don't sweat *that* much!

My hydration pack had sprung a leak. All 3 litres had dripped away. It must've happened at the beaver pond, I figured, when I sat down against that rock.

Why did I sit down with my back to a rock? Why didn't I take off my hydration pack first?

Stupid-Stupid-STUPID, I thought. Ultra stupid.

It was 31 degrees and as humid as a sauna. The next rest stop was 7 miles away.

I opened the pack and peeked inside. I had maybe 3 millilitres of water left in there.

Want to know the definition of screwed — 3 millilitres of water is the definition of screwed!

I drank those 3 millilitres and considered my options.

I could keep moving and hope to reach Grace Point. Of course, I'd probably get heatstroke and fry to a crisp before I got there.

I could sit down in the shade and wait for another runner.

They might give me a gulp or two of water, but probably not much more.

Or, I could drink the water from Hither Lake. It looked clean, and I'm sure it would have tasted great, and for 2 or 3 miles, I'd probably feel fine. But then my stomach would start to grind, and my intestines would turn to liquid. And for the next 2 days I'd be exploding from both ends.

It's called beaver fever and it's like the flu, only worse. The beavers poop in the lake; that's what makes you sick.

Idiot, I thought. Why hadn't I noticed that my water pack was leaking? If I'd noticed sooner, I could have conserved my water, instead of sucking it back whenever I felt thirsty.

I walked for 20 minutes, hoping another runner would come along. Of course, no one did. What happened to the Dirt Eater, I wondered? Maybe Kneecap was right; maybe he'd dropped out of the race.

My throat felt as dry as a chalkboard eraser. The water in Hither Lake was looking more delicious all the time.

I pulled out Kneecap's phone. I started texting my mom. But what could I write that wouldn't freak her out?

Another sign: Mile 39. In the last 2 hours I'd run 4 whole miles.

Four miles in 2 hours. That meant I was going 2 miles an hour. Lame!

I sighed and sat down in the shade beneath a tree. And then, thank God, the bandit came along.

At first I thought he was talking on a headset, but when he got closer I realized that he was just mumbling to himself. He was hunched over and looked like a human comma.

His face was deeply tanned — the colour of an old boot.

He looked up and saw me. "Hello there, Mr. Scheurmann," he said.

He wore a floppy hat and a baggy T-shirt that said *IT'S NOT LUCK* across the front. He had to be as old as my grandpa.

"Hi," I said. "How do you know my name?"

He stopped running and put his hands on his hips. "You're Tom's son, right?" he asked. I nodded. "I heard that you were running the race. Not many kids your age out here, so I figured it had to be you."

His sunglasses were massive. As big as a car windshield. He seemed to be looking at a spot above my left shoulder.

"Did you fall?" I asked.

His legs were caked with mud. A bloody gash ran down his right forearm. "Oh yeah," he said. "I was trying to keep up with a very fast runner girl." He smiled to think of it. "We could probably still catch her if we tried."

"Did she have a bear bell attached to her shoe?" I asked.

The old guy nodded. "Now that you mention it, she did," he said.

"That's not a girl," I said. "That's Kara."

"Well now, of course she's not a girl to you — she looked to be in her forties or maybe fifties — but that's plenty young for me."

His body shook as he bent over and laughed. His laughter sounded like water gurgling down a drain.

"Do you have any extra water?" I asked.

He took off his hat and ran his hand through his grey hair. "You ran out? Out here?"

I felt my face go hot. The old guy stood up straight. Well, not exactly straight. Straighter. He looked at me for a few seconds and then shrugged off his knapsack.

"Lucky thing I came along," he said, unzipping his pack and pulling out a wineskin. "Take a gulp of this."

It wasn't water, but it was cool and delicious. "Whoa," I said. "That's intense."

"My own secret recipe," he said.

It was like drinking a Christmas tree. It was like swallowing a thunderstorm on a hot summer night.

"A lot of antioxidants in that," my visitor said. "Rosewater, mint, basil — it's real good for your kidneys."

I drank and drank while the old guy told me about himself. I couldn't stop.

"I used to play for the Edmonton Royals," he said. "You've probably heard of me . . . Kern Gregory, Number 1? The Holy Moly Goalie from Muskogie?"

This seemed to matter to him a great deal, so I lied and told him that his name sounded familiar. He'd done me a huge favour, letting me drink from his wineskin, so I figured I owed him one.

"Hydration's the most important thing," Kern said, "both in hockey and in running. You can train all you want, but if you don't keep hydrating, you're toast. Hey, you don't look so good, if you don't mind me saying. Take another hit of the magic water . . . "

He pushed the wineskin back at me. The more I drank, the more I wanted. Suddenly I felt like I was going to throw up. Luckily, it turned out to be a belch.

"Whoa there," said Kern. "Take it easy."

I wiped my mouth and took a few deep breaths.

"If it's any consolation," he said, "everyone out here feels just as lousy as you do. You don't run a hundred miles without getting beat up. But we didn't sign up for a luxury cruise, now did we?"

That laughter again. The guy loved to laugh.

I gave him back his wineskin. I'd drunk at least half of the magic water, but Kern didn't seem to notice.

"Feeling better?" he said. "That's good, that's good."

My fanny pack made a trilling noise.

"Is that a phone?" Kern asked.

"Yeah." I pulled it out and read the text. Another GO QUINN GO! from Ollie. Only, he'd misspelled it. He'd typed GF QUINN GF! To me, it looked like GOOF QUINN GOOF!

"Can I borrow that for a second?" said Kern.

"Sure," I said, handing him the phone. "Can I have a little more water?"

"You're still thirsty?"

"Actually . . . " I told him about my hydration pack.

"Jeez!" Kern said. "Why didn't ya say so?" He reached into his knapsack and pulled out a plastic jar with a tube attached to one end.

"What's that?" I asked.

He grinned. "It's another brilliant save by the Holy Moly Goalie from Muskogie! This, my dear boy, is a water purifier!"

He plucked my empty water bottle out of its holster. Then he walked down to the edge of the lake. "This'll take a few minutes," he said, and I watched as he filled up the plastic jar. He pumped the water through the filter and into my bottle and then he dropped in a purifying tablet and shook it up.

"We'll let that sit for a few minutes," he said.

I stared at my bottle, now full of delicious, almost-drinkable water, while Kern tapped and double-tapped the screen of Kneecap's phone. "My daughter's running this race too," he said. "She's somewhere ahead of us, and I'm curious how far she's got."

I sat in the shade and looked out at the lake. I felt like the luckiest person in the world. A water purifier. What were the odds? I'll bet no other runner had brought one of those along.

Kern squinted at the screen. "She's passed Grace Point," he said. "Hey, she's doing all right."

"Why aren't you running with her?" I asked.

Kern frowned. "Too slow for her," he said. "Besides, I'm not even supposed to be in this race. I never got around to registering."

That explained why he didn't have a number. "You're a bandit," I said.

Kern said nothing, but pointed at my bottle. "That should be safe to drink now," he said.

I drank half the water down and instantly felt better. Kern walked back to the edge of the lake. He filled the purifier a second time and began pumping the water through the filter.

"You know what I love more than anything?" he said, looking out at the lake. "I love seeing the sun come up two or three times in the same race, and knowing that I haven't been to bed once."

He refilled my bottle for the second time. "There ya go," he said. "Don't drink that one too quickly. It should be enough to get you to Grace Point. It's only six more miles, but we'll stick together just in case. They should have an extra hydration pack that you can borrow."

We ran together for the next hour and a half. Kern was slower than me, but I didn't mind going at his pace. He told great stories, which made the time pass more quickly and distracted me from my aches and pains.

"Bruce said that every race has a surprise," I said. "I guess that leaky water pack was my surprise, eh?"

"Oh, I don't know," said Kern. "That was just a little malfunction. I think the real surprises are the things we learn about ourselves."

We came to a tree that had fallen over the trail. I ducked under it. Kern took his time climbing over.

"What do you mean?" I asked.

Kern reached into his pocket and pulled out a granola bar. He broke it in two and passed one of the halves to me.

"Most people don't even know why they're out here," he said. "They don't know if they're running *to* something, or running *from* something."

I thought about this for a few moments. "What if someone isn't doing either?" I asked. "What if he's, you know, just *running*?"

For the first time since we'd been together, Kern turned and looked me right in the eyes. "Then they're blessed," he said.

Blessed, I thought? What does that mean, *blessed*?

All of a sudden, Kern began to laugh.

"What's so funny?" I said.

"I don't know!" he cried. "I'm just feeling giddy. Everything seems funny when you've run forty-three miles!"

The trail markers led us down the side of a steep ravine. I flew right down, but Kern took it more slowly. When he got to the bottom he told me to run on ahead.

"We're almost at Grace Point," he said, pulling out his compass and stepping off the trail. "I can't stop there since I'm not registered, so I'm going to go backcountry for the next couple of miles."

"Want me to grab you some food?" I asked.

"Nah, I've got a dozen sandwiches in here . . . " He patted his knapsack as if it were a pet. "Just don't forget to ask Bruce for an extra bladder for your hydration pack. Oh, and if you happen to see some of those cookies with the red jam in the middle . . . "

"You like those things?"

"Who doesn't?"

Ummm. Just about everyone.

I promised Kern that I'd grab him a dozen. It was the least I could do after he'd saved my life.

But they didn't have any of those cookies at Grace Point. Not that it would have mattered. I didn't see Kern again until after the race.

GRACE POINT

Mile 45

I left Kern behind and followed the trail to the edge of Hither Lake. Waves crashed against the beach, and strips of snow-white foam bobbed on the water like dotted lines on a highway. I ran along the shore, following the pink flags, and 5 minutes later I cruised into Grace Point station. Hip hop was blaring from a pair of speakers, and volunteers were mixing jugs of powdered sports drink.

A round-faced man in a Japanese kimono sat me down on a plastic chair.

"No," I said. "I don't want to sit down." Beware the chair, I was thinking.

The kimono guy paid no attention. "Massage!" he said.

"Who, me?" I said.

He grinned. "You bet!" He draped a towel over my shoulders and pressed his thumbs into my neck.

"Yowch!" I shouted.

"Relax," kimono guy said.

I did. It still hurt. Then, all of a sudden, it felt great.

My head rolled backward and I started to groan.

"You're drooling, brother."

"Sorry," I said.

He wedged his thumb beneath my shoulder blade and pressed. Fifty thousand volts of electricity shot through my eyes. A moment later, the pain melted away, and my body glowed with a liquid warmth. "That feels good," I said.

"Thanks!" said kimono guy.

I was starting to smell a bit rank, I noticed.

"Sorry I'm so sweaty," I said.

"I'm used to it," kimono guy laughed.

I have no idea why people volunteer at 100-mile races. They have to put up with some pretty disgusting stuff. For instance:

> BO
> Repulsive blisters
> Rude and exhausted runners
> Gatorade breath
> Evil-smelling T-shirts and socks
> Lots of talk about vomit, pee and poo

When the massage ended I thanked kimono guy (*"Domo arigato!"*) and floated over to the food table, feeling as loose as a jellyfish. I ate a cup of the most delicious chicken noodle soup, except that it wasn't really soup. It was full of beans and shredded carrots and it was as thick as chili — it was more like chicken noodle chili.

A red truck pulled into the parking lot. Bruce climbed out. I charged straight over.

"Lucky Number Thirteen!" he said. "How you doing?"

"Pretty good," I said. "But my hydration pack is toast."

Bruce's eyebrows popped up. "Spring a leak?" he said.

"Yeah," I said. "Have you got any extras?"

Bruce led me over to the supplies table. He bent down and pried open a cardboard box. "We should have something in here," he said. "Yours holds three litres, right? Hey, look at this . . . "

He pulled out what looked like a plastic IV bag and tube.

"Aha," he said, popping off the lid. "It seems clean." He smelled the inside. "Well, clean enough."

He filled it with water, screwed the lid shut and squeezed. There didn't seem to be any leaks.

SAVED!

Kneecap's phone rang. I recognized the number.

"Hey, bro," I answered. "Where *are* you guys?"

Ollie didn't answer my question. Instead, he deafened me with a "GO QUINN GO!"

"Hey, buddy!" I said. "How's my pacer?"

"GO QUINN GO!" he yelled again.

While I'd been losing my marbles and chatting with storm clouds, Ollie had been having a very productive day. In the 10½ hours it had taken me to run 45 miles, he'd caught three frogs, helped Mom buy an antique butter box, played six games of Crazy Eights, eaten a half-dozen Nanaimo bars and made it to Level 8 on his favourite video game.

"Sounds like you're having a great day," I said.

"I am!" he said. "Hang on — Kneecap wants to talk to you."

There was a moment of silence. I thanked Bruce for the bladder, and wandered down toward the lake.

Kneecap came on the line. "Yo! Q-Tip!" she said.

"Hey," I said, "you survived your mountain-climbing adventure."

"Yeah, and guess what? I was right about that guy with the neon socks."

"You mean the Dirt Eater?" I said.

"He was still sitting in that lawn chair when I got back down. I bet he's STILL sitting out there."

A smudge of green caught my eye. A water snake was swimming across the tops of the waves.

"Where are you?" I said. "I just got to Grace Point, but I can't wait around for you guys forever."

"Something's wrong with your car," said Kneecap. "We're stuck at the nastiest gas station in the world. Hang on — your mom wants me to give you a message. She says, Sorry about missing you . . . We'll catch up to you at Ratjaw . . . "

I smiled. "Tell her it's okay," I said.

I stared at the lake while Kneecap passed on my message. The snake cut through the water like a knife through butter. I suddenly felt sad. I felt a lump in my throat. I hadn't realized how much I was looking forward to seeing them.

"Hey, how are you doing, anyhow?" Kneecap asked.

"I'm okay," I said.

"Okay, or okay-ish?"

"Ish," I said. "I'm slowing down. I ran the first twenty-three miles in four and a half hours, but it took more than six to run this last twenty-two."

Kneecap snapped her gum. "Stop it," she said. "You just ran forty-five miles. That is huge, don't you realize that? It's epic. Heroic."

I sighed and said nothing.

"You're doing great, Quinn," she said. "So stop worrying, okay? Hang on, here's your brother."

The snake slid into a pile of rocks on the shore. Ollie came back on the line.

"Hey again," he said.

"Hey again," I said. "Can you tell me a joke?"

Ollie was silent for a moment. "A knock-knock joke, or a real joke?"

"A real one," I said.

There was a long pause. I kept watching for the snake.

"I don't think I know any real jokes," Ollie said finally.

"Sure you do," I said. "Dad used to tell them all the time."

I wandered back to the food table with the phone pressed to my ear. I ate a chunk of banana and washed it down with ginger ale.

"I could tell you a story," said Ollie.

"What story?"

"About the time Mom told a lie."

"I don't tell lies," I heard Mom say in the background.

"Yes you do," said Ollie. "You did once, anyway."

He started in on the story of our family trip to New York. I remembered it perfectly, of course. It had only been two years since we'd flown there, back when Dad ran the New York City Marathon. Mom signed me up to volunteer at a water station. It was my job to hand out paper cups of water and Gatorade to the runners. My water station was near the end of the race, close to Central Park, which I knew from TV.

We got to the water station early in the morning, hours

before the first runners arrived. Ollie and I climbed all over the statues in the park while Mom helped set up the stretcher tables and mix the Gatorade. Around ten o'clock, everyone started cheering. The first-place runner was coming down the road. Ollie and I scrambled to the curb and watched him sprint past. He didn't take any water from anyone. He didn't even smile when people yelled his name.

A bunch of other runners was right behind him. They were small, thin men — from Africa, I think — and their faces were scrunched up with what looked like concentration and pain. They'd run 23 miles in less than 2 hours. I had no idea people could run that fast.

A few minutes later a woman ran past. She didn't stop to drink anything either.

"See her?" said Mom. "That's Paula Radcliffe."

"Who's Paula Radcliffe?" asked Ollie.

"The fastest woman in the world," said Mom.

Paula's blond ponytail bounced back and forth as she ran. A TV truck drove beside her, filming her every step.

A few minutes later, more runners went by. They were still very fast and their faces were clenched, but some of them reached out to take a cup of water. They drank as they ran, or poured the water over their heads. It was November and all the volunteers were wearing jackets, but the runners looked like they were pretty hot.

I asked Mom when Dad was coming.

"Later," she said, laughing. "Much later."

The trickle of runners became a stream, and then the stream became a river. Now all the runners wanted something to drink. The volunteers stood in a long line at the edge of the road, holding out our paper cups, yelling "Water!" or "Gatorade!" A lot of cups got dropped, and everyone got splashed. It was loud, and crazy, and the most fun I've ever had.

The runners were all shapes and sizes now. They were skinny, chubby, muscular, old. A woman with a metal leg ran past. She bounced like a gazelle, and everyone cheered. A guy went by, juggling three balls. A man in a pink ballerina costume. A girl dressed as a clam.

The minutes passed by, but Dad didn't come. I started to worry, but there was no time to worry — I was too busy shoving cups at all the runners. There were zillions of them now, and most of them stopped to walk when they took their cup of water, and everyone tossed their empty cups to the curb. Volunteers swept the cups into massive plastic bags, but as fast as they worked, they couldn't keep up with all the garbage.

"You're almost there!" Mom yelled at the runners. "Only three miles left! You can do it!"

Some of the runners flashed a thumbs-up sign. Others frowned and stared hopelessly at the road.

The pavement was wallpapered with flattened paper cups. Lots of the runners looked pretty beat-up. They were limping and gasping for breath and their eyes looked like cracked marbles. And then, all of a sudden, there he was.

"Hey, kiddo," Dad said.

He was sweaty, red-faced, yellow-shirted. Ollie ran up to him and hugged his white legs.

"Hey there, buddy," said Dad. *"Yowch!"*

Ollie had accidentally stepped on his foot. Dad sat down on the curb and untied his shoe.

"What happened?" Mom asked.

His right sock had been replaced by a tensor bandage.

"What, this?" Dad said. "Nice fashion statement, eh?"

He tried to laugh it off, but you could see that he was hurt. He massaged his foot with his hands.

"You're looking good," said Mom.

"Don't lie," Dad said. He wasn't smiling.

Mom looked at his foot. "So," she said again, "what happened?"

"The usual," he said, glancing around. "How far away did you park the car?"

Mom didn't answer. The crowd kept cheering for the runners. "You're quitting?" she said at last.

"Yeah, my race is over," said Dad.

A woman came off the road and lay down on the grass. Paramedics rushed over and took her blood pressure and checked her eyes.

Dad unwrapped his foot. The bandage was the colour of milky tea.

"Does it hurt?" Mom asked.

"You bet it does," said Dad. "Hey, Ollie, give me one of those." Ollie had opened a pack of Fruity Juicers. Reluctantly, he handed one to Dad.

Mom said, "You know that we're in New York, right?"

She sounded angry, which made Dad look up. "Of course I do," he said. "Why?"

"Only because you've been talking about this race since the day I met you. You always said you wanted to run the New York City Marathon. You never said you wanted to run three-quarters of it."

Dad unwrapped the Fruity Juicer and popped it into his mouth. "It's not like I have a choice, hon," he said. "I'm not cut out for running on pavement."

Mom stared at him. "What do you mean, you're not cut out?" she said. "You've got two legs, don't you?"

"Yes, but — "

"And they're not broken, are they?"

"No, but the pavement is harder than the trails back home and — "

"Don't listen to your pain," Mom said. "Listen to your heart. Your heart wants to finish this race."

Dad shook his head and clicked his tongue. That was bad. He didn't do that very often.

"It feels like I've got a knife in my foot," Dad said. "You have no idea how much pain I'm in."

"I gave birth to two ten-pound boys," said Mom. "Do you think it's maybe as painful as that?"

Dad glared like a rattlesnake eyeing a frog. "I said I'm quitting," he repeated.

"Fine then." Mom turned to Ollie and me. "Come on, kids, let's go. You won the bet after all."

Me and Ollie looked up at her, surprised. Mom zipped her purse and stood up.

"What bet?" said Dad.

"The kids bet me that you wouldn't finish," said Mom, fishing the car keys out of her pocket.

I was shocked to hear her say those words. Not only was it a lie, it was mean!

"I'm sorry, honey," Mom said to him. "But you're absolutely right. Twenty-six miles is a crazy distance to run on pavement. It's a miracle anyone finishes this race at all."

Dad looked like he'd been hit over the head with a hammer. "Come on, boys," Mom said. "It's a long walk to the car."

Dad glowered at the three of us. Then he began winding the tensor bandage around his foot. "I know what you're trying to do," he grumbled.

"Is that so?" said Mom. She was holding Ollie by his shoulder. "What is it, exactly, that I'm trying to do?"

Dad drank a cup of water. Then he took a deep breath and pulled his shoe back on. He tied it, stood up and began walking down the road. His face was as red as Mom's beet borscht.

"See you at the finish line!" Mom shouted. A hint of a smile tugged at the corners of her mouth.

Dad started to trot. "Have the divorce papers ready!" he shouted back. And then he was lost in the rainbow of spandex shirts.

Dad crossed the finish line an hour later. He was one of the last runners to receive his medal. He was in a lot of pain, but I'd never seen him so happy. He hoisted Ollie onto his shoulders.

"I lied," said Mom. "The kids never really made that bet."

* * *

"And that was the day Mom told a lie!" said Ollie.

"Yeah, but she did it for a good reason," I said.

"Still," said Ollie. "A lie's a lie."

"Give me the phone, young man," I heard Mom say.

She came on the line a moment later. She sounded testy and tired. "Hey," she said.

"Hey," I echoed.

"I'm sorry we're not there," she said. "This stupid car . . . It's your dad's fault. I told him not to buy an import."

A big wave crashed against the shore. I sat down on a rock that was shaped like a chair.

Mom said, "We'll catch up to you at Ratjaw, I promise."

"Don't worry about it," I said. "I'm fine on my own."

"I know," said Mom. "Sometimes you're *too* fine on your own."

The telephone line whistled between us. "Listen, Quinn," she said finally, "I need to say something important."

"Okay," I told her.

She took a deep breath. "You know how, when you step on a wad of gum on the sidewalk, it sometimes gets stuck to the bottom of your shoe? And you can't get it off no matter how hard you try?"

"I guess so," I said.

"That's what family is like," Mom said. "It can be messy and annoying, but it's impossible to scrape off."

A cicada droned and then suddenly stopped. The phone bleeped, and the battery icon shrank by one bar.

"Is that all?" I asked.

"That's it," said Mom. "No matter what happens, you're stuck with us."

A snake slithered through the grass at my feet. It had different colours from the one I'd seen in the water.

"Do you understand what I'm saying?" said Mom.

"I think so," I said.

Then, because the wind was rattling the cedar branches, I asked my mom a very strange question. "Mom," I said, "can you think of anything that doesn't have a shadow?"

She didn't even need to think about it. "That's easy," she said. "The sun."

"Oh . . . yeah," I said. Why hadn't I thought of that?

"Wait a minute," said Mom. "I thought of something else."

"What?"

"A mother's love. Because it's even brighter than the sun."

"Come on, I'm being serious," I said.

"So am I," Mom said. "My love is brighter than a disco ball. It's brighter than Albert Einstein covered in glitter . . . "

"Mom. *Please*. Don't make me throw up."

"I love you too, young man. See you at Ratjaw. Run safe!"

IN EVERY RACE THERE IS A SURPRISE

Mile 51

You'd think that after running for 12 hours, throwing up, nearly dying of thirst and hallucinating so badly I started talking to storm clouds, the worst of my troubles would be behind me.

You'd think that. But you'd be wrong.

Bigger troubles still lay ahead. For instance, I wrote my obituary at 6:10 p.m. That's right — my obituary. My death was moments away.

QUINN SCHEURMANN, 1999–2013. Passed away suddenly during the annual running of the Shin-Kicker 100-Mile Race. Cause of death: mauled by bear. Charges of negligence are pending against race organizers . . .

Too bad I wouldn't live to see it in print, I thought. Unless I could pull off a miracle in the next 3 seconds.

What was it my dad had said about bears?

> *If it's black, attack!*
> *If it's brown, lie down!*

You weren't actually supposed to attack black bears. But if you scared them well enough, threw rocks and made noise, they were supposed to chicken out and run away.

Brown bears, on the other hand, were trickier. Most brown bears are grizzlies, and grizzlies aren't scared of anything. The only thing grizzlies are afraid of is missing dinner. If you run into one of them, Dad advised me, then play dead.

Unfortunately, this bear wasn't black or brown. Instead, it was a rusty shade of orange. Worse, it was as big as a fridge. It was standing on its hind legs. And yes, it was growling.

Bears are fun to see at a zoo, or at the side of a road, when you're safe inside a car. But when you're running through a forest, all alone, miles from civilization? Seeing a bear then is a total drag.

Crap, I thought. This totally sucks. Not only might I die at any moment, but I'd finally started making decent time. For the last hour I'd been running along the edge of a lime-stone ridge. The trail was hard and flat and fast. It was like running on a superhighway.

Suddenly I heard stones clattering right behind me. Something was huffing and puffing. I jerked my body to a stop.

The bear was shaggy and monstrous and boy did it stink! A swarm of deer flies buzzed around its head.

I clenched my butt cheeks to keep my guts from spilling out. I expected the bear to charge, but instead it dropped onto all fours. It rubbed its head against a rock and made a snuffling noise with its nose. Its smell was truly awful. It stank like wet dog.

SYDNEY WATSON WALTERS: Please tell me that you got away from that bear.

QUINN: I didn't. Because there's one little detail I haven't mentioned. The bear was wearing camouflage pants.

SYDNEY WATSON WALTERS: Camouflage pants *again*? So the bear was another hallucination?

QUINN: Exactly. Number two, in case you're counting.

There is nothing quite as hilarious as a bear wearing pants. I stifled a giggle. It's Winnie the Pants, I thought.

The bear shook its head and took a few steps backward. Then it lay down on its back and rolled around in the dirt. Its snout was pebbled with raspberry seeds, and its eyes drooled like a sea lion's. Did I mention that it was huge? Way bigger than a fridge! More like the size of an SUV.

"Where'd you get those pants, Mister Bear?" I asked.

The bear rolled over and shook out its fur like a puppy that's been swimming. It raised a paw to its snout. "Shhhh," it said. Then it rose up on its hind legs and placed its front paws on my shoulders, as if it were about to give me some fatherly advice. It leaned way down, until its black snout was a centimetre from my forehead. It took three deep sniffs and let out an epic sneeze.

"Thanks for that," I spluttered. "I needed a shower anyway."

I wiped the bear snot off my face while Winnie the Pants dropped back onto its four paws.

"Um," I said. "Where are you going now?"

The bear twitched its ears and made a chuffing noise. Then it made a movement with its paw, as if to say, "Follow me."

I decided to follow. I mean, c'mon! How often do you get to hang out with a bear in tight pants?

We went down a narrow path and dropped beneath the cliff. Hither Lake, far below us, glinted like shiny nickels.

The path turned, and I saw a curtain of water. The bear glanced back at me. It held out its paw.

It took me a minute to see what it was pointing at, but eventually I noticed the hole in the rock. For a moment, I forgot that I was running a race, and tore down the path to check out the cave. The mist from the waterfall fogged up my sunglasses. I yanked them off and stuffed them in my pocket.

The first thing I noticed about the cave was the cold. It felt like someone had left a freezer door open! The ground was uneven, and the rock walls were covered in moss. A gap in the rocks let in a grimy pool of sunlight.

I walked inside. In the dim light, I saw a very strange thing. A grey female turtle was sitting in a shallow hole. I know it was female because it was laying an egg.

"Whoa," I said. "That's gotta hurt."

The turtle's eyes bulged. It didn't seem to care that I was there. Twelve fist-sized eggs were glistening in the hole. As I watched, a thirteenth egg rolled to the bottom of the pit. It was grey and coated with stringy slime.

"Hey, that's amazing!" I said, looking down.

The turtle looked exhausted. Its eyes were prehistoric. It scratched the ground with its foot and flipped some dirt over its eggs.

"Careful," I whispered. "You'll get them dirty."

The turtle tilted its head up at me and glared. Then it blinked its eyes and turned back to its eggs, nudging them into a circle in the bottom of the nest. They sat on a blanket of spongy leaves and branches. I could see shreds of plastic bag and swatches of fabric in there too.

"Hey," I said. "What's that?"

I pointed at a yellowed scrap of paper. The turtle nudged it with its beak-like jaw, and I reached down and grabbed it.

"Thanks," I said.

The turtle crawled up the side of its hole and began kicking at the dirt again.

"Hey!" I said. "What are you doing?"

It flung the earth with powerful back legs, which were shaped a bit like shovels. "Those are your eggs," I said. "You're getting them dirty."

Snapping turtles, I found out later, bury their eggs. But at the time I thought this one was just being stupid.

"They're your babies," I said. "Don't you care about your babies?"

Apparently not, since it kept shovelling the dirt.

Feeling depressed, I walked back to the mouth of the cave. The bear had ambled in behind me and was sitting on its rump. It stuck out its tongue and licked its black lips. Then it snuffled the air and made a popping sound with its jaw.

I sat down on the ground and looked at the newspaper clipping. The headline said: *Local Runners Hit the Wall*. There was a black-and-white picture of a kid with skinny legs. "Wait a second," I said, "that's me!"

It was a story about the Seawall Shuffle, a 10-kilometre

race they hold every year by the ocean. My dad and I ran that race last summer, but the course was super crowded, and we lost each other while we ran. Dad crossed the finish line 20 minutes after me, which is an eternity in a 10-kilometre race.

"Boy, are you ever slow!" I told him.

"Not my fault!" said Dad. "Didn't you see the whale?"

He claimed that he'd seen a blue whale from the seawall. He even showed me pictures he'd taken. "It's right there," he insisted. "That dark line, can't you see it?"

I could see the dark line, but it didn't look like a whale. So I never knew if he was telling the truth.

"Why would I lie about a whale?" Dad asked.

"Because you're embarrassed about running so slow," I said.

Now I knew the truth. The newspaper story mentioned the whale, which swam close to the seawall and caused a lot of excitement. "Hundreds of runners stopped to take pictures," the article said, "rather than chase after a personal best."

The bear grunted and popped its jaw. Then it walked to the edge of the cave and rubbed its forehead against a mossy rock.

I looked at the picture in the centre of the story. Me and my dad are holding up our finishers' medals, and grinning.

My watch beeped. It was 7 p.m. now. I stuffed the article into my pocket.

I walked to the back of the cave. The turtle had filled up its hole and was tamping down the dirt.

"You really did it," I said. "You buried your eggs. You buried the things you love the most."

The turtle stopped moving. Its eyes were shiny and wet.

"That's a pretty weird thing to do," I said.

Golden sunlight streamed into the cave, lighting up dozens of spiderwebs. They were everywhere, strung up between the cave's craggy pillars. In the centre of each one, I could see a big, fat spider. The spiders sat hunched in their webs like greasy black fists. A cloud passed in front of the sun and the webs all disappeared.

The turtle lay down on the ground and closed its eyes. I realized I was intruding. So I disappeared too.

SUNSET AT RATJAW

Mile 61

SYDNEY WATSON WALTERS: So how were you feeling, after that experience?

QUINN: Pretty freaked out, I have to say! I kept reminding myself that the bear and turtle were just hallucinations. By the time I got back to the main trail, I'd calmed down a bit.

SYDNEY WATSON WALTERS: And what about your super-powers? How were they holding up?

QUINN: My muscles were sore, but I wasn't out of breath. And I was still running pretty fast. I knocked off the next 10 miles in 2 hours.

SYDNEY WATSON WALTERS: Is that what they call being "in the zone"?

QUINN: Yeah. Everything felt perfect. But it didn't last long.

I rolled into the Ratjaw rest stop sooner than I expected. It's near the tip of Catfish Point, at Mile 61. I crossed the highway and picked up the trail on the other side. I could see the parked cars and picnic tables at Ratjaw, a hundred metres down the path.

Then I heard the air brakes.

An eighteen-wheeler was cruising down the highway. The driver geared down as he rounded the curve. I thought the truck would keep going, but it didn't. Instead, it slowed down and pulled over to the shoulder. The driver stuck his arm out of the window and waved. "You're not running in the hundred-miler, are you?" he shouted.

I nodded.

He shook his head. "How far have you come?"

"Sixty-one miles," I called back.

The passenger door opened and clapped shut. Someone hopped out on the other side.

The truck driver grinned. "You're awesome!" he said. "I can't even run to the corner store!"

He waved again and threw the truck into gear. The tires kicked up a cloud of dust.

As the truck pulled away, I saw someone standing in the dust. He was wearing a black T-shirt and neon socks.

The Dirt Eater! He was back in the race! But he hadn't *run* here; he'd hitched a ride!

He crossed the highway, acting totally innocent. No way was I going to let that happen!

"Hey there!" I called out. "How's it going?"

His eyes were flamethrowers. "Going fine," he sneered.

He walked right past me, limping slightly.

"Have fun, riding in that truck?" I asked. "Was there a sleeper in the cab? Did you take a nap?"

I was being what my mom would call a brat. The Dirt Eater didn't answer. What could he say?

"I'd love to take a nap," I went on. "Oh, wait — I can't — I've still got thirty-nine miles to run."

The Dirt Eater spun around. "Do me a favour," he snarled, "and shut your yap."

He glared at me for about 30 seconds. Then he said, "You've got more lip than sense."

While I tried to figure out what to say next, the Dirt Eater loosened the drawstring on his shorts.

Whoa! Time out! Very bad form!

You do not pee in the middle of the trail! Not when another runner is right behind you! You walk a few metres into the forest to do it. If that's not an official rule in ultra running, then it should be, starting now.

I was about to say something especially snotty, but I figured I'd already made him mad enough. So I ploughed through a patch of waist-high grass, making a wide arc around the Dirt Eater and his pee.

"That's right, Monkey Boy," he said. "Leave the angry old man alone."

Creepy, I thought. And I started to jog. I wanted to get far, far away from that guy.

The volunteers cheered when they saw me coming. "Number Thirteen!" someone shouted. "Way to go!"

A thin woman led me to a folding chair.

"Sixty-one miles in fourteen hours," she said. "Not too shabby."

I sat down and sipped from my hydration pack. I thought about reporting the Dirt Eater, telling the volunteers how

I'd seen him climb out of a truck, but I decided to keep my mouth shut. I was here to run a race, not to be a rat. If he wanted to cheat, then that was his problem. Besides, the volunteers were writing down when each runner came and went from every rest stop. If anyone checked, they'd see that the Dirt Eater's times didn't add up. You didn't have to be a math genius to figure that one out.

"You look good," the woman said. "How are you feeling?"

"Not so good, to be honest."

I hadn't noticed any pain while I'd been running, but now that I'd stopped, I could feel it kicking in.

"What hurts?" the woman asked.

"Everything," I said. "My stomach sort of sucks. My shoulders are brutal. And my feet are really giving me hell."

"They're giving you *what*?"

I looked up at the woman. Realized who she was. "Heck," I said. "They're giving me heck."

"That's better," said Mom.

I teetered forward and gave her a hug. A stinky, sweaty hug that no one else would have taken.

"Let me see those feet," she said.

"Nah, they're okay," I said. "I was just kidding."

A total lie. My feet felt like they'd been dipped in gasoline and set on fire. I hated to think what they must look like.

"It wasn't a request," said Mom. "Let me see them — *now*."

Just then the Dirt Eater jogged into the rest stop. The same people who'd cheered for me now cheered for him.

"Where's Ollie?" I asked, changing the subject.

"Down at the lake with Kneecap," said Mom.

She was still looking at my feet. I needed to distract her.

"I want to thank you," I said.

"For what?" she said.

"For your genes," I said.

"My genes?"

Mosquitoes dive-bombed my ankles and shins. I rifled through my pack for the bug dope I'd packed. "I inherited your good bones," I said. "I wouldn't still be standing after sixty-one miles if I didn't."

"Is that so?" said Mom.

"That's so," I said.

I was laying it on thick, but I didn't care. She seemed to have forgotten about my feet.

"You got some of your dad's genes too," she said. "You definitely inherited his determination. But he was a plodder — terrible form. You're different. You run with such grace — like a springbok."

A springbok is an African version of a deer. I didn't know that then, but I pretended that I did.

"You're doing very well, you know," Mom said. "At this rate, you might even beat your dad's record."

The bald guy in the kilt was walking toward us. I had to think hard to remember his name.

"Hey, Quinn!" he said. "How's that bladder working?"

Bruce. That was his name — Bruce.

"It's great," I said. "I'm drinking a ton! My pee is so clear! Want to see?"

That made him grin. "No thanks," he said. "Come on over. It's time for your weigh-in. You know the drill."

I climbed up on the scale. The screen lit up.

"You've dropped two more pounds," Bruce said.

"Two *more*?" said my mom.

Bruce shrugged. "He's only lost three, which is average. There was a fella in here earlier who was down eleven. I had to pull him out of the race."

I thought to myself: I was in sixth place before. But if Bruce pulled one of the leaders, that meant I was . . .

FIFTH!

"Still," said Mom. "Three pounds, that can't be good."

The volunteers began clapping. The Dirt Eater started running down the trail. Now he was ahead of me, in fifth place, and I was back to being sixth.

"Wow," said Bruce. "He made a good recovery."

I stepped down off the scale and said nothing. I'd show them who owned fifth place.

* * *

You probably think you've seen some nice sunsets. But this sunset was amazing. This sunset was on steroids!

Half of the sky was the colour of ripe watermelon, and the rest blazed orange, like a melting scoop of sherbet.

On the downside, the bugs were launching an attack. The volunteers pulled on hoodies and long pants and lit citronella candles.

I walked down to the lake, stinking of bug dope. Kneecap was skipping stones. Ollie knelt beside a bush.

"Hey there," I said.

"Shhhh," said Ollie.

Kneecap smiled at me. "He's frog hunting," she whispered.

A blood-red sunbeam shot through the clouds and stained the cedar trees a dark shade of purple.

"Is it a bullfrog?" I asked Kneecap.

"A leopard frog, I think."

"No," said Ollie, "it's a *Bufo americanus*. And if you don't keep quiet, he'll never come back up."

The three of us stared at the black water. A light breeze blew across the lake.

"They're calling for rain tonight," Kneecap said.

"Great," I said. "Bring it on."

Kneecap looked at the clouds on the horizon. Then she said, "I bet the Dirt Eater is in bed by now."

"No, he's not," I said. "He just ran through here."

"Not possible," she said. "He was hours behind you."

I told her about the truck on the highway. Her eyes went wide. She had dog-dish eyes.

"WHAT?" she said. "You saw him climb out of a *truck*? He must've hitchhiked from Silver Valley. What is wrong with that guy?"

Two eyeballs appeared on the water's surface. Then a tiny nose and two webbed feet. The frog paddled slowly toward the shore. All at once, Ollie sprang into action.

"Gotcha!" he cried, dropping his hands over the frog. He lifted it up so we could take a look.

"He doesn't look too happy," I said, peeking between my brother's thumbs.

"I'll let him go in a minute," said Ollie.

The frog scowled like an indignant king, angry at having his schedule interrupted.

Kneecap slapped a mosquito on my neck. "How do you

feel about running in the dark now?" she asked.

"I'm a bit spooked," I said. I was terrified, actually.

"Me and Quinn ran in the dark together once," Ollie said.

"Really?" said Kneecap.

"You bet," I said, winking at Ollie. "We're a team."

The sun dipped below the horizon. The sky looked as if it had been smudged with charcoal. Ollie set the frog down on a mossy rock. It hopped back into the water with a splash.

"I wrote another verse for the UHL anthem," I told Kneecap.

Kneecap's face lit up. "Sing it for me!"

"Okay," I said.

> *Our school is proud and strong*
> *Especially the second-floor john*
> *That's where we belong.*
> *Our teams are bold and free!*
> *With streams so extraordinary!*
> *Number one and unsanitary!*
> *God save our league!*

Kneecap's smile broadened and then slowly collapsed. "It's great," she said. "But the UHL's dead."

"I know," I said. "But maybe we can revive it."

She considered this. Then she said, "Nah, it's had its day. It was a childish game, anyway."

We followed the sound of laughter back to the rest stop. At the picnic table I found my drop bag among the others and yanked on a fresh shirt and my nylon jacket. I strapped my headlamp to my forehead. I also loaded up on banana-flavoured gels, jelly beans and a small spool of duct tape.

"What's the tape for?" Ollie asked.

"In case my shoes get ripped," I said.

Kneecap ran over. "I just talked to Bruce," she said. "I asked him how the Dirt Eater could possibly be beating you."

"What did he say?" I asked.

"He said that Ted — that's the Dirt Eater's name — is an experienced runner. And they rely on the honour system in this race."

"What's the honour system?" Ollie asked.

"It seems to mean that you can cheat all you want and not get caught," muttered Kneecap.

Why would anyone cheat like that? It's not like he had a real shot at winning the race. The fastest runners were probably hours ahead of us by now. They might even be close to the finish line.

Ollie helped himself to a handful of pretzels. "When will you pass the Shrine?" he asked.

"Soon," I said. "A little over thirty miles."

Ribbons of campfire smoke wafted through the trees. The glow of an mp3 player lit up Kneecap's face.

"It's my bedtime soon," Ollie said. "I won't be able to tell you any more stories."

"Then tell me one right now," I said.

Ollie knelt down to tie his shoelace. "What kind of story?" he asked.

"A true story," I suggested.

Ollie pressed some pretzels into his mouth and sucked the salt off them. I clipped on my hydration pack and took a squirt of water.

"One time, last summer, I had a toad," Ollie began. "I caught him under the climbing tree behind our house."

I remembered this. "You named him Tony," I said.

"Yeah, Tony. I kept him in my aquarium. I put grass and leaves in there. Fed him bugs. Sometimes a cricket."

"One day I took him out of the aquarium and let him hop around the backyard. River was there."

River's our neighbour's dog. He's big and sleepy-eyed and he has incredibly bad breath.

"Anyway," said Ollie, "Tony was hopping around on the grass, and River was lying close by, sort of watching, but not really. Then Tony decided to hop between River's front paws. River leaned forward to sniff him. Tony took another hop forward. River went to lick Tony, and then Tony hopped right inside River's mouth!"

Ollie scratched a mosquito bite on his leg.

"Why was River's mouth open?" I asked.

"Because he was sticking out his tongue! And Tony just hopped into the hole!"

It was a horrifying story, but it was also kind of funny. "What happened then?" I asked.

"River looked surprised, like he was going to throw up. Toads don't taste very good, you know. He shook his head and Tony popped out of his mouth and rolled across the grass. He was shiny from River's slobber, but aside from that he was okay. I scooped him up really fast, and he peed all over my hand."

I stared at the blue light fading over the lake.

"So what happened to Tony?" Kneecap asked. She'd taken off her headphones and was sitting up on the bench.

"I set him free," Ollie said. "He wanted to get home to his family."

A burst of laughter erupted behind us. The volunteers were drinking beer and telling stories around the fire. Mom was standing apart from the other people. I glanced at our car, the silver hatchback, and for a moment I imagined myself sliding into the passenger seat. I'd ease the seat back and rest my head against the window. I'd probably turn on the fan, and warm air would blow in my face as I slept . . .

Kneecap saw what I was looking at. "Don't even think about it," she growled.

I took a deep breath. "Right," I said. And then I ran into the forest before I had a chance to change my mind.

"Don't forget to keep singing!" Ollie shouted after me.

"Scare away the bears!" Kneecap added.

DO NOT LOOK INTO THE WOODS

Mile 67

SYDNEY WATSON WALTERS: What was it like, running in the forest at night?

QUINN: Weird.

SYDNEY WATSON WALTERS: Scary, I'll bet.

QUINN: Definitely. And really, really dark.

All my life I'd heard stories about the Sasquatch. Not to mention Freddy Krueger and the Blair Witch. I'd always thought that those stories were lame. But now, they didn't seem lame at all.

I had gone night running with my dad before. But I'd never done it by myself. In those first few minutes after the sun went down, I was pretty freaked out. I wanted to dig a hole at the side of the trail and lie down and cover myself with leaves. I wanted to bawl my eyes out until I felt better.

I admit it. I was so scared that I wanted to cry. I wanted my mom. I wanted to go home.

I didn't give up, though. Instead, I kept running. Just like I'd been doing for the last 15 hours.

Just keep going, I told myself, and maybe you'll forget that you're scared . . . I never forgot, though. I always felt scared. The terrified feeling never went away.

For the first few miles, the trail followed the shoreline. A full moon came up and coated the lake in silver light. Chimney Top, which was now almost 40 miles behind me, glowed pale blue.

Thousands of moths flew toward my headlamp. A cloud of mist swirled around my legs. There were lots of stream crossings, and I had to be careful not to trip over fallen logs or tree roots. Somewhere, far off, a firecracker exploded.

I took Ollie's advice and sang my lungs out. I sang the commercial for Albert's Pancake House. Then I sang "Lose Yourself" by Eminem, and songs by Troutspawn:

> *He would lie down on train tracks!*
> *Set his ponytail on fire!*
> *He was a sky-diving BASE jumper,*
>   *on the attack.*
> *The adrenalin took him higher!*

My dad went to see Troutspawn in concert once. He said the lead singer wore a traffic cone on his head and a sparkly suit made of tinfoil.

"Me and my buddies loved them," Dad told me. "Their songs sounded like they were from a different universe. We thought they were such a weird band, we used the word

Troutspawn as an adjective. When something was really sick, we'd say it was Troutspawn. When something was bizarre, we'd say, "That's so Troutspawn!"

My favourite Troutspawn song is called "Rope to the Sky":
> *You got bike spokes in your stomach*
> *And your veins are full of stones*
> *And did you need to fill your 'hood*
> *With all those broken bones?*

The song's rhythm is perfect for running. It's got 180 beats per minute, the same speed my legs like to go.

I sang "Rope to the Sky" for an hour or so, until the temperature dropped and I started to feel cold. I checked my watch — it was 10:37 p.m. I kept my eyes peeled for the tiny pink flags. They were planted in the ground, 200 metres apart.

Suddenly, right behind me, I heard a loud *crack*! I spun around. Saw the flash of a headlamp.

"Who's there?" I demanded.

"Your worst nightmare!" someone shrieked.

The headlamp blinded me and for a second all I could see was a yellow-green halo. Two invisible arms pulled me into a hug.

"Hey there, Lucky Number Thirteen!" said the voice.

My heart was a jackhammer and my hands were curled into fists. "What the heck are you doing?" I shouted. "You scared me to death!"

Kara laughed. "Sorry about that. I would've shouted earlier, but I was enjoying your singing."

I was still half-blind from the glare of her headlamp, and embarrassed that she'd heard my lousy voice. "What are you doing behind me?" I shouted. "You should be at the finish line by now."

"I got lost," Kara said. "I zigged when I should have zagged. Did an extra loop around Ratjaw."

"An extra loop?" I said.

"Yeah," she said. "I lost the trail somehow. I figure I ran five extra miles."

She laughed to think of it.

"When did you figure out you were lost?" I asked.

"When I noticed that I was running through a lot of spiderwebs. They were catching me right in the face. The only way you should be running into spiderwebs in a race is if you're in first place, which I knew I wasn't. So the only other possibility was that I'd gone off the trail. It took me about an hour to figure that out."

"Spiderwebs are disgusting," I said. "They come out of a spider's bum, did you know that?"

Kara laughed. "I suppose that's true, isn't it? Hey, Bruce said I'm in seventh place, so you must be sixth. Have you seen any lights up ahead?"

"No," I said. "But the guy ahead of me is a cheater."

I told her about the Dirt Eater. "Is he the guy with those crazy socks?" she asked.

I nodded.

"Yeah, that dude looked shifty to me," she said.

The moon, I noticed, had changed colour. It was now as orange as the inside of a cantaloupe.

"What happened back at Luther Marsh?" Kara asked. "I turned around and you were gone."

"I bonked," I said. "I needed to lie down." I decided, for

the moment, not to mention my conversation with the Wind.

Kara was still wearing a tensor bandage around her knee. "How's your leg?" I asked.

"Iffy," Kara said. "Your stomach?"

"Better," I said. "But now my feet hurt."

"We're running a hundred miles," said Kara. "Something *always* hurts."

She took a plastic bag with little white pills out of her fanny pack. "Need something for the pain?"

"No thanks," I said.

She swallowed two pills and then put the bag away. "I saw your friend Kneecap back at Ratjaw," she said.

"Did you see my brother?"

"The little guy? He's a cutie. He told me he's your pacer."

"He was," I said. "But it's past his bedtime."

"That's okay," Kara said. "You and I can pace each other."

We continued running. I took the lead, and Kara followed. The light from my headlamp splashed ahead of me into the forest. At one point we ran near a waterfall. The gurgling water was close to where we were standing, but when I shone my light around, I couldn't find it.

"Don't be doing that," said Kara.

"What?" I said.

"Don't shine your light into the forest."

"Why not?" I said.

"Just trust me," she said.

The temperature continued to drop. I was still wearing shorts and I was feeling the cold. I kept dreaming about the next rest stop. I had a drop bag there, crammed with tights, gloves and a hoodie, and I'd packed a chocolate bar. The thought of that chocolate bar made my mouth water.

"How far to the next rest stop?" I asked.

"Come What May? About sixteen miles."

Oh, man, I thought. At my pace, that meant 3 hours of running — at least.

"Why's it called Come What May?" I asked.

"Because once you pass beyond it, you're completely on your own. All the other rest stops have road access, but not that one. The only way to get there is on horseback, or ATV."

"Or on foot," I added.

"That's right," said Kara. "But nobody would do that. That would be crazy!"

We laughed and kept running. The pain in my feet got worse and worse. It felt like I was running on thumbtacks — thumbtacks that had been dipped in acid. It felt like the soles of my feet had been shaved off with a rusty chisel. It was incredibly painful. Ultra painful.

Flash! A firefly lit itself ablaze and hovered between the trees like a green, glowing eye.

"That's cool," I said.

"Look, there are more."

We stopped for a moment and switched off our headlamps. All around us, fireflies blinked on and off. The forest was almost totally silent, and I thought I could hear the clicking of the fireflies' wings.

Kara flipped her headlamp back on. "Want me to take the lead?" she asked.

"Sure," I said.

We ran some more and the pain got worse. It felt like a rattlesnake had bitten my feet, and the venom was racing up my legs. With every step, my brain screamed, Ouch, ouch, ouch, ouch, stop, stop, stop!

"I need to walk for a while," I told Kara.

"Okay, we'll walk then."

For a moment we both strolled along. But it didn't feel right.

"No," I said. "You should run."

Kara turned to face me. "No can do," she said.

"Why not?" I said. "Because I'm a kid?"

"No," said Kara. "Because you're a friend."

A warmth spread through my body when she said that. Still, I felt guilty for slowing her down.

"Listen," I said. "I know that you're a cop. But trust me on this. I'm totally fine."

"I don't mind going slow," Kara said. "It's a wonderful night for a hike."

I reached out and grabbed her arm. "No," I said. "If you're feeling good, you have to keep running. You didn't enter this race to hike. You could still win this thing."

I didn't mention my secret agenda: I wanted her to beat the Dirt Eater.

Kara stared at me for a very long moment.

"Trust me," I said. "I'll be fine. My feet hurt, that's all. I just need to walk for a while."

"Are you absolutely sure?" she said.

"Absolutely," I said. "Just promise me you'll beat that cheater."

Kara grinned and gave me a hug. Then she set off down

the trail. I watched the light from her headlamp bounce back and forth between the trees. Bit by bit, it got smaller and smaller. It disappeared, reappeared and then finally blinked out completely.

For a moment I felt like I was going to cry, I was so sad to see her go. "Kara!" I shouted.

No answer. No sound.

Kara was gone.

No, not gone, I told myself. She couldn't be more than a half mile down the trail.

I walked and walked. The shadows around me seemed to vibrate.

To keep from getting scared, I sang:

> *Go ahead, just stare out that window*
> *At the night that tears you to shreds.*
> *There are other heads to turn,*
> *other bridges you can burn,*
> *And the moon, she can bring back*
>   *the dead,*
> *Yes the moon, she can bring back*
>   *the dead.*

Another Troutspawn song. I must've sung it for an hour. I wondered what creatures in the forest were listening to me.

Just keep the legs moving, I told myself. Don't think about the creatures.

Maybe an hour later, I slipped and fell onto a rock. When I sat up, my hands were wet and sticky. Blood.

I sat on the ground for a few moments, giggling. My head hurt. My feet throbbed with pain.

"Kara!" I shouted. "Kara!"

Nothing.

"Dad!"

The crackle of twigs. A flurry of moving branches. Something was creeping around in the forest.

I forced myself back to my feet. Soon the rest stop will appear, I told myself. And after that, the finish line. Just keep moving forward. Just keep the legs moving. Soon the pain will end and the scars will heal.

I pushed on. Light from my headlamp flickered across the ground, and shadows shrank behind the trees. Sometimes it looked like the shadows were alive, and I realized that my brain wasn't working quite right. My thoughts darted back and forth between the real world and make-believe, and it was getting hard to know which was which.

I thought about Kern, the bandit. He'd said that people were either running *from* something, or *to* something. And if they weren't doing either, then they were blessed.

I wondered what I was. I sure didn't feel blessed. And I wasn't running to anything, since my future mostly looked like crap.

Did that mean I was running away from something? If so, what was it? Could I ever outrun it?

The trail began climbing a long, rocky hill. It seemed to go up for miles and miles. I stopped and ate a banana-flavoured gel and a handful of jelly beans. A needle of pain shot up my leg. My left hamstring felt as tight as a bicycle spoke, so I sat down on a stump and massaged it for a few minutes. I looked up from where I was sitting and saw a sign that said Mile 70.

Just 30 miles left, I told myself. Thirty miles — that

wasn't very much! Just a marathon plus another 4 miles. Easy-peasy!

I stood up and limped forward. Another hour passed. The moon disappeared. The sky filled with mist.

Then something exploded beside my foot.

PLOOOOF!

It was as loud as a thunderbolt. There were three more explosions.

PLOOOOF! PLOOOOF! PLOOOOF!

Holy frack! What was that!?

Something ran screaming through the leaves. I spun and saw three cabbages run across the ground. The cabbages had stumpy wings. They zigzagged crazily between the bushes.

My heart stopped, then slowly rebooted. I knew what these were.

"Stupid birds!" I muttered. "You're lucky I didn't step on you!"

The wild turkeys clattered away into the forest. My heartbeat slowly returned to normal.

Another hour passed. The sky turned as black as tar. At a certain point, I noticed that I stank.

"You reek, buddy," I muttered to myself. "You smell like sour milk. With rotten cucumber thrown in."

Keep the legs moving. Keep the legs moving.

My back hurt. It felt like someone had whacked it with a crowbar. Still, I kept running. Well, sort of.

Keep the legs moving. Keep the legs moving. And whatever you do — do not shine your light into the forest.

At some point, a memory came into my head. A memory from when I was 3 years old. I remembered this cat named

Zeus we used to have. He was old and asthmatic and he wheezed loudly when he slept.

One night I begged Daddy to let me take Zeus for a ride in my stroller. Daddy said okay, but you'll have to hang on to him tight.

Daddy lifted Zeus into the stroller beside me and then he rolled us down the smooth asphalt driveway on Champlain Drive. I cuddled Zeus in my arms as if he were my baby, and he purred like Mom's sewing machine as we rolled down the sidewalk. The stroller had rubber wheels that went *ka-thlump ka-thlump* as they rolled over the sidewalk cracks. The sky was as blue as our recycling box, and I could see the whole sweep of it behind Daddy's face as he ran.

Keep the legs moving. Keep the legs moving.

Zeus. Me. Daddy. The blue sky. I smiled at the memory and rolled my head sideways.

Instantly, the light from my headlamp played across the trees, and four yellow eyes stared back at me.

Two of the eyes were level with the ground, but the other two were high up in the trees. A cougar, maybe? Getting ready to pounce? The eyes blinked and went out. The ones on the ground kept staring at me.

A bolt of fear shot down my spine. I pointed my headlamp back down at the trail and kept running.

Keep the legs moving. Keep the legs moving!

Finally, when I thought I couldn't run any farther, a pinprick of green appeared down the trail. I ran toward it. It bobbed back and forth between the trees. It was a glow stick, dangling from a tree branch!

I ran farther down the trail and saw another glow stick. There was another one after that, and then another one after that.

Ten minutes later, I saw the light of a campfire. Somebody zapped my eyeballs with a flashlight.

"Runner!" a familiar voice cried out.

It was the most delicious sound I'd ever heard.

COME WHAT MAY

Mile 83

It was two in the morning and I was still on my feet. I'd been running (and power walking) for 20 hours.

Two people clapped as I hobbled into the checkpoint. A horse whinnied somewhere in the darkness.

"You're looking fresh!" a woman said.

"Don't lie," I growled.

A lantern was burning on a picnic table, and above it, a disco ball hung from a tree branch. The light from the lantern bounced off the twirling ball and fractured into a thousand pinpricks of light.

The woman took my water bottle and refilled it from a plastic keg. She was young and pretty and her hair was the colour of a banana. "I'm Kaylin," she said. "And you must be Quinn."

I nodded but didn't say anything. My brain was too fried to come up with an answer.

"I'll bet you're starving," said Kaylin. "What can I get you?"

Two pots were bubbling on a camp stove. The propane gas made a high-pitched whistle. "I've got soup and lasagna," Kaylin said.

"Maybe in a couple minutes," I said. All I wanted was that candy bar in my drop bag.

A short-haired man was sticking logs on the fire. I nearly fell over, suddenly realizing who he was. "What are you doing here?" I said.

He looked up. "Hey, kiddo," he said.

I rushed over and he hugged me tightly. It was like being wrapped in pure sunshine. I instantly felt warmer, feeling the bulk of his belly.

"But how the heck did you get *here*?" I said.

"I grabbed a late flight," he said.

I drank in the sight of him. The disco lights swirled across the backdrop of trees. This couldn't be happening — not really.

"What's wrong?" said Dad.

"You can't really be here," I said. "It's not possible."

He laughed. "Nothing is impossible," he said. "You should know that better than anyone. You're running a hundred miles in one day. Most people would say that was impossible."

He took my hand and led me toward a chair.

"No," I said. "I can't sit down."

"Why not?"

"Bruce told me to beware the chair."

Dad chuckled. "Don't worry about that," he said. "I'll make sure you get up and running again — that's a promise."

I sat down for the first time in what felt like weeks. It felt better than my birthday and Christmas morning put together. I stretched my hands toward the fire. The warmth of those flames was sweeter than sleep.

Dad knelt down on one knee and poked at the fire with a stick. The shadows of the flames licked grooves into his face.

"So you're telling me you flew here?" I said, still not really believing it.

"Sure did," he said.

"And how was your flight?" I asked.

"Long," he said.

He had pebbles for eyes and his usual brush cut. He looked a bit older than I remembered.

"How long can you stay?" I asked.

"How long do you want me to stay?"

"Forever, of course!"

Dad laughed. I knew he couldn't stay.

I looked over at Kaylin, who was standing behind the stove. She smiled and stirred her pot of soup.

"Anything wrong?" Dad asked.

"I'm cold."

Dad unclipped my hydration pack and pulled it off my shoulders and refilled it at the plastic keg.

Meanwhile, I fumbled to open the zipper of my drop bag. I dug out my two extra shirts and my pair of tights, that chocolate bar I'd been dreaming of and my weatherproof gloves. Then I zipped up my drop bag and sat back down by the fire.

Dad came back. His smile was slanted.

"What?" I asked.

"I wish I was running this race with you, that's all."

"You can run the rest of it for me if you want," I said. "I've had enough of this crap. Here, take my bib."

I began pulling the safety pins out of my shirt.

"Don't," said Dad. "No one can finish this race but you."

"But I don't want to finish," I said. "This whole thing is so stupid."

Dad re-pinned the racing bib onto my shirt. "I know we were supposed to run this race together," he said. "I'm really sorry that didn't happen."

He gave me back my hydration pack. I tried not to feel sad. I thought about all the times Dad and I had run the trails near our house. All the times he'd farted and blamed it on me.

I pulled on my extra shirts. Then, after checking to see that Kaylin wasn't watching, I yanked off my shoes and shorts and pulled on my tights. This took a long time, since my fingers felt like slugs, but I finally managed to get them up to my waist.

I unwrapped my candy bar. Dad took out a cigarette.

"You started again?" I asked.

"Yeah." He pulled a book of matches out of his pocket and stared at it for a long time. Eventually he tossed the cigarette into the fire and picked up a bag of licorice instead.

"You've run eighty-three miles in twenty hours," he said. "You're doing all right, Quinn. Better than all right."

"I suppose so," I said. "At least I'm not dead. Yippee for me. Here's to not being dead."

"Yippee for you," Dad agreed. He turned his camp chair so we were facing each other. The smoke from the fire blew between us and made him look cloudy. He not only looked older, he looked thinner too.

"You've still got your sense of humour," he said.

"I don't know," I said. "Kneecap called me a fun vampire."

Dad nodded and opened the bag of licorice. "I know it's hard," he said. "But when this is all over, I bet you'll think this was a great adventure."

I wasn't sure if he was talking about the race anymore. I took a bite of my candy bar. I wanted to tell him how much the race sucked and how much I hated him for making me sign up. But instead I said, "I've still got seventeen miles to go. That's only one, two, three, four . . . Wait. I've forgotten how to count that high."

Dad gripped the plastic armrest on my chair. "I know it hurts," he said. "But pain can be good. Pain is how we learn. If you're not feeling any pain, then you're not learning anything."

What the heck was he talking about now? "My butt is killing me, Dad," I said. "My cheeks feel like two sheets of sandpaper rubbing together. And my knees — holy cow! It's like someone unscrewed my kneecaps and poured gravel in the holes. Plus, I've been hallucinating. I had a conversation with the Wind."

Dad stared at the fire and nodded. "Did it say anything important?" he asked.

Kaylin stopped stirring her pot and looked over.

"It asked me to help look for its shadow," I said.

"But the Wind doesn't have a shadow," Dad said.

"I know that," I said.

Dad bit the end off a licorice twist. A light from the disco ball flashed across his face. "I used to hallucinate too," he said.

"You did?"

He nodded. "Last year at Western States, around mile sixty-two, I washed my face in a stream and saw a monkey grinning back at me."

Somewhere, that horse whinnied again. I shivered.

"I used to see buildings in the forest too," Dad went on. "Factories, houses, mosques with minarets."

I didn't know what a minaret was then. But I pretended that I did.

"Are hallucinations dangerous?" I asked.

"Nah." He took another bite of licorice. "They're just a reminder to eat more sugar." He held out the bag. "Want one?"

"No thanks," I said. "I've eaten too much sugar. I'll be pooping cotton candy if I eat any more."

Dad nodded and went on chewing. I reached down and pulled off my socks. My feet were swollen and grey and lumpy, like oatmeal.

"Wow," said Dad. "That's impressive."

Four angry blisters — each one larger than a toonie — lit up the soles of my feet.

"What should I do?" I said.

Dad shrugged and turned back to the fire. Kaylin wandered over. "Let me see those puppies," she said.

"That's okay," I said. "My dad'll patch me up."

"Who?" Kaylin said.

I looked around but he'd disappeared. He must've gone off to pee in the woods. Kaylin knelt down and looked at my feet. "Nice," she said, sucking air between her teeth. "I need to treat these blisters — right now."

Treat them? "How?" I said.

"Don't worry," said Kaylin. "I'm trained in first aid."

She filled a basin with water and squirted some dishwashing soap into it and sloshed the water around. She washed my feet and then she popped the blisters with a pin. I guess I must have screamed a bit.

"Don't worry," she said again. "I've seen worse."

She dried my feet with paper towels. Then she took something long and thin out of her pocket.

"What's that?" I asked. It was a tube of Krazy Glue.

"Runner's best friend," Kaylin said.

She squirted a blob of glue into each blister. Then she pressed the flaps of skin together.

"Good as new," she said, spooling duct tape around my feet. Then she pulled my socks and shoes back on and re-tied the laces.

I tried standing up. My feet didn't hurt as much as before. They felt like they'd been smeared with clay and were starting to harden.

"Okay now," said Kaylin. "Before your body goes into shock, I need to get some food into you."

"I already had a chocolate bar," I said.

"That's not enough," said Kaylin. "When's the last time you had some real food?"

I looked at my watch. "I had some PB & J back at Ratjaw almost five hours ago."

"Then you need to eat. Like I said, I've got lasagna and chicken noodle soup. What'll it be?"

"I'll take the soup, I guess."

Kaylin walked back to the picnic table.

"She fixed your feet, huh?" Dad said, surprising me.

Somehow he'd materialized beside me. I fought back the urge to ask him where he'd been.

"Yeah," I said. "They feel a bit better. Thanks a lot for all your help."

Dad ignored my sarcasm. "Did she give you something for your chafing?" he asked.

"My what?"

"Your butt cheeks. You said they felt like sandpaper."

My face went hot. "I didn't tell her about that," I said.

"Don't be embarrassed," Dad said. "It happens to all runners. Just ask her if she has any ointment."

"No way," I said. "I'll survive."

A log on the fire crackled, and the sparks flew high into the air. Dad followed them with his eyes and then kept staring at the sky.

"You're passing through a hallway," he said.

What the heck was that supposed to mean? "I'm sorry?" I said.

"You've closed a door on one part of your life," Dad said, "but you haven't opened the door to the next room yet. You're in a hallway, waiting for the next thing to happen. Don't worry, another door will open soon enough."

I didn't have a clue what he was talking about. Dad smiled, but it wasn't a happy smile.

Kaylin came back over with a cup full of soup. The noodles were crunchy, but the salty broth was good.

"By the way," Kaylin said, "you're in sixth place."

That's weird, I thought. I'd been in fifth place at the last rest stop, but two people — Kara and the Dirt Eater — had passed me.

"Are you sure I'm not seventh?" I said.

"Nope," said Kaylin. "One of the leaders dropped out."

"Who, Kara?" I said.

"Oh no, she came through here an hour ago. She looked great. She was flying."

I thought of something. "Was it the guy in the *Eat My Dirt* T-shirt?"

"You mean Ted," said Kaylin, her lips pressed tightly together. "No, he was looking strong too."

I wondered how Kern, the bandit, was doing. But he was running in secret, so I didn't mention his name.

Kneecap's phone vibrated. I pulled it out of my belt. It read: GO QUINN GO!

"What's that?" asked Dad.

"Ollie must be awake," I said.

I held the phone up so he could see the text.

Dad smiled. "It's getting late," he said. He looked at me meaningfully. "It's time you got out of that chair."

"I don't want to go," I said. "It's so warm here." My fingers and toes tingled in the warmth of the fire.

"You have to start sometime," he said. "You've got a long way left to run."

"Thanks for reminding me."

Dad put another log on the fire. It sizzled and roared to life.

"Maybe I'll DNF," I said. "You wanted to DNF in New York, remember?"

"I was injured," Dad said.

"I'm injured," I said.

"Where's your injury?"

"Here." I pressed my hands to my heart.

Dad poked at a burnt log with a stick. "That'll heal," he said. "That thing is stronger than you think."

He handed me a plastic bag filled with nuts, chips and chocolate cookies. Then he pulled me to my feet.

"You can do anything you set your mind to," Dad said. "And don't forget, you still need to visit the Shrine."

I pulled my hydration pack over my T-shirts. My body felt as stiff as an ironing board. I looked down the trail. It was blacker than a black hole. It looked as if someone had taken a picture of a black hole and smeared black shoe polish all over it.

"You really want me to go in there?" I asked.

Dad winked at me. "You're a terrific kid," he said. "Have I told you that lately?"

I shook my head and set off, jogging slowly. My body crackled with pain. The chicken soup sloshed inside my belly.

"This is the stupidest thing I've ever done!" I shouted. "I'm never doing this *ever* again!"

I expected my dad to reply with something funny, but instead Kaylin shouted, "Don't give up!"

Her voice sounded far away, as if she were underwater. I turned around to wave, hoping to see my dad, but the rest stop had vanished, and all I could see was the darkness.

ANOTHER SURPRISE
Mile 88

Somewhere over the next few miles, things started getting tough.

I know I've made it sound like things were tough already. But things were about to get ultra tough.

For instance, at Mile 85, I ran headfirst into a tree. I crumpled to the ground, my forehead gushing blood, and for a few minutes I just lay there, giggling in the dirt.

Then, at Mile 86, my headlamp started flickering.

Great, I thought. Just what I need! If my batteries died, I'd be stuck on the trail all night long.

I slapped my headlamp, and the light stopped flickering and grew brighter. Awesome! I thought. But how long would it last?

At Mile 88 I reached the toughest stretch of all. It began with the train tracks and then it got worse.

The train tracks ran along a high, narrow ridge, and it was instantly obvious that they weren't used by trains anymore. Shrubs and sawgrass grew between the rails and some small trees were growing between the cross ties.

The trail markers ran along the edge of the tracks, so I walked between the rails for a while. The cross ties were a foot apart — too close together to run comfortably on — so I hopped up on the rail and tightroped along that. It was tricky, and I kept falling off, so after a while I gave up and went back to jogging along the edge of the tracks. The rail bed curved south, glowing blue in the light of the moon. The trees on both sides of me waggled in the breeze.

Another beep from my watch. It was now 3 a.m. I began switching back and forth between running and walking. I'd walk until I got cold and then I'd run to warm up, and when my legs couldn't run anymore, I'd go back to walking again. My headlamp was still shining brightly, thank God. Why hadn't I been smart enough to bring extra batteries?

Suddenly I noticed that the trees on either side of me were gone. The bushes and sawgrass had disappeared too. I flashed my headlamp all around. What happened to all the trees? I wondered.

I figured it out eventually. At some point, without noticing, I'd started walking across a bridge. Now I was standing on a span above a pitch-black valley. I looked down at my feet. Thick, tarry-smelling beams ran crosswise beneath the tracks. There were gaps between the beams, and nothing underneath.

I dropped to my knees and crawled to the edge of the track. There was no railing there, just a sudden drop. I reached down and picked up a pebble from one of the cross ties, dropped it over the edge and watched it disappear into the void. I didn't hear it hit anything down below.

What the heck was Bruce thinking? I wondered. A runner could easily trip and die out here!

I crawled back to the middle of the tracks and stood up. I flashed my headlamp forward and backward. I couldn't see any trail markers.

That's when it hit me. Crap, I thought. I'd gone off the trail! I wasn't supposed to be on this bridge at all!

A spear of ice shot through my heart. I was all alone. In a forest. In the middle of the night. And I was lost.

Relax, I told myself. Stop freaking out and THINK. When was the last time you saw a pink flag?

I couldn't remember. Was it before I reached the tracks, or after? I was starting to hyperventilate. I couldn't remember anything. Calm down, I told myself. Breathe deeply. You'll find your way back to the trail.

But would I? I was lost and scared and bleeding and hungry. All I could think of was how much I wanted some of those toast soldiers that Dad used to make every Sunday.

Dammit, I thought. Why hadn't I eaten some of Kaylin's lasagna at the last rest stop? I'd have given anything for a mouthful of that now.

Chill out, I told myself. Breathe deep.

SYDNEY WATSON WALTERS: Sounds like you could've used your pacer just then.

QUINN: For sure. I kept telling myself to chill out, breathe deep. It didn't do a lot of good, though.

SYDNEY WATSON WALTERS: Why didn't you just turn around and walk back along the bridge to solid ground?

QUINN: Because that would have been the smart thing to do, and as you already know, I'm not very smart. If I'd retraced my steps I would've eventually found the pink flags. But for some reason, that thought didn't occur to me.

SYDNEY WATSON WALTERS: You'd been running for 21 hours, so I think we can cut you some slack. But what did you do to get out of that mess?

I walked farther out onto the trestle. I was curious to see what was on the other side of the gorge, so I walked for 20 metres and then suddenly I stopped.

My foot was sticking out over nothing. The iron tracks were shorn off and the bridge simply ended. Broken timbers stuck out in all directions. There was nothing in front of me but a 200-metre drop.

Whoa! I thought. Ever heard of a guardrail?

I sat down and swung my legs over the edge and stared down at the canyon that had nearly become my grave. I took out my bag of yogurt-covered cranberries and tossed them, one by one, into the abyss. What had happened to the bridge? I wondered. Had it collapsed while a train was passing over? If so, what had happened to the people on the train? Was I looking down at their bones right now?

Weird, I thought. One moment you could be riding on a train, looking out the window at the passing trees and lakes, and the next moment, for no other reason than really crappy luck, you could be plunging into a gorge, living out your last moment on earth.

I promised myself I'd never get on another train. And certainly not a plane. Or a boat. Or a car. Or a bike.

From now on, I'd run wherever I needed to go. Running was the safest mode of transportation ever.

But then I thought: That is SO not true. Just look at how many times I'd nearly died today!

My watch beeped, signalling the time. It was 3:30. I swung my legs back and forth. The wind blew cold air down my back, and for a moment I considered letting myself slip off the edge of the bridge. That's how miserable I felt — like a nickel that's been placed on the tracks and flattened into a smear of tinfoil by a passing freight.

I felt dead. Ultra dead.

I squinted at the far side of the gorge. I thought I could see a grey blanket of trees. They seemed to be whispering in the breeze. And then, far away, I heard the train.

"Mwaaaaaaaaaaaaaaaaaaaaaaaaaa!"

It was hard to hear over the sound of the wind. At first I thought it was my imagination.

"Mwaaaa-Mwaaaaaaaaaaaaaaaaaa!"

No doubt about it — it wasn't my imagination. It was coming closer. But it can't be, I thought. The bridge is out.

"Mwaaaa-Mwaaaaaaaaaaaaaaaaaaaaaa!"

Still closer, I thought. But something wasn't right. It didn't sound quite like a train.

"Mwaaaaa-Mwaaaaa-Mwaaaaaaaaaa!"

The noise echoed off the canyon walls. It sounded more animal than machine. And it was coming from below.

"Mwàaaa-Mweeeeeeeeeeeeeeee!"

I crawled back from the edge of the bridge and poked my headlamp between the cross ties. A black shadow drifted beneath the trestle. It was massive, the size of a submarine.

"What the heck is that?" I whispered.

"MWAAAAAAAOOOOOOOOOOOOOO–AAAAAAAA–
IIIIIIIIIIIIEEEEEE!"

It was bigger than twenty school buses caught in a net. It was a blue whale, swimming up from the bottom of the gorge.

This is *so* not happening, I thought.

But it was.

The bulk of its body rose up above the bridge, and a huge watery eye blinked down at me. The whale slapped its flipper against the tracks and rubbed its barnacle-encrusted head on the sharp end of the trestle. Eventually, it floated in beside the bridge, lowering its back down to my level.

"Nice parking job," I said.

The whale waggled its tail fluke, and the whole bridge shook. It would have been so easy for me to climb onto its back.

Just then, the moon stepped out from behind a cloud and sprayed a rainbow of silver rays over the clearing.

"The moon can make rainbows?" I asked.

The whale didn't answer.

It was a rainbow without colour. A moon-bow. A ghost-bow. It was the strangest, most beautiful thing I'd ever seen.

The whale twitched its flipper again. Then it started singing.

Saaaaaaay helllloooooooooooooooooo!
Waaaaaaave gooooodbyyyyyyyyyyyye!

Yes. The whale was singing in English. Which made it official: My mind was falling apart.

"Please don't," I said, putting my hands over my ears.

Of course the whale ignored me and carried on.

Swiiiiiiiiiiiimmmm tooooodaaaaayyyy!

Tooooomoooorroooow weee flyyyyyyy!

My headlamp flickered. My breath felt ragged. The leaves of the poplar trees hissed in the breeze.

Wait a second — the leaves of the poplar trees hissed in the *breeze*!

For the first time in hours, I remembered the promise I'd made to Wind.

"I need to ask you a question," I told the whale.

The whale stared at me with its huge watery eye.

"Wind's shadow," I said. "Do you know where it is?"

Lightning flashed in the distance. Cold air stabbed my neck.

The whale drifted up and down beside the trestle.

"I know it doesn't make sense," I said. "I mean, I know Wind is invisible. So she can't even block the light."

A flash of orange lit up the edges of the sky. Thunder sounded far away.

The whale rolled sideways and sank down a couple of metres. Its tail remained perfectly level with the bridge.

"You want me to climb on to your back, don't you?"

The whale's huge tail moved slowly up and down. Just one step — that was all it would take.

"It's tempting," I said. "But you're just a hallucination. It's a long way down if you're not real."

The whale didn't speak, but I read the meaning in its eye. *Sometimes you have to trust*, it said.

Lightning flashed in a corner of the sky. It was only a matter of time until Wind came back.

SYDNEY WATSON WALTERS: Please tell me you didn't step off that train bridge . . .

QUINN: *(Says nothing)*

SYDNEY WATSON WALTERS: You did? But the whale was just a figment of your imagination.

QUINN: Oh, I know that now. But it sure felt solid enough at the time.

SYDNEY WATSON WALTERS: Great. You climbed on to the back of an imaginary whale. And what does a whale's back feel like?

QUINN: Like the skin of a mango that isn't quite ripe. I could feel its beating heart through the duct tape on my feet.

I sat down with my legs folded and my chin pressed against my knees. My heart was beating faster than a baby squirrel's.

That lightning again. It was coming closer. The night sky was milky; the colour of a blind dog's eye. And then I felt the thrashing of the tail.

The whale and I rose into the air and angled away from the bridge. Everything got blurry as tears streamed from my eyes. Below us, the world was racing with shadows.

The whale went into a dive and we plunged toward the trees. And then, for what seemed like hours, we swam through the forest. I clung to a mound of barnacles on the whale's head to keep from sliding off, flashing my headlamp from side to side.

But as hard as we searched, we didn't find Wind's shadow. I was beginning to suspect that Wind never had one in the first place. Why did it matter so much anyway? I wondered. Looking down, it was clear the whale didn't have one either.

* * *

When I woke up, I was back on solid ground, lying beside the train tracks and a line of pink flags. I looked at my watch. It was 3:33. Three minutes had passed.

I suppose you could say that the thing with the whale was just a dream. But it would be wrong to think that it didn't happen. Something happened to me in those 3 missing minutes. I learned that there's more than *one* type of shadow.

I stood up and started running. I felt completely recharged! I hadn't felt this good in hours.

I ran and ran, glancing up at the moon-bow as I went. It looked like a frozen river in the sky. The beam from my headlamp was stronger than ever. My mind felt clear. My superpowers were back!

Wind is invisible, I told myself. That's why it doesn't have a shadow.

But invisible things have different kinds of shadows. That's what I realized on the back of the whale. Nightmares, for instance. They cast shadows inside your brain.

And stories, also invisible, throw shadows on your heart.

The trail dropped into a ravine and followed a creek. The glow of my headlamp lit up the rocks in the water.

And what about love? I asked myself. It's invisible too, but it casts a very long shadow. It can make you feel safe when you're lying in bed, but when it leaves, it hurts worse than a tooth that's been pulled.

I shone my headlamp down at the rushing water. The

rocks beneath the surface looked like grinning skulls.

The ravine broadened out at Hither Lake, and I saw huge waves heaving themselves against the shore. The silver moon melted and turned sickly green. The moon-bow darkened and disappeared.

No doubt about it, I thought, love has a shadow. The bleakest and angriest shadow of them all.

The moon swam through sooty clouds. Another wave crashed against the rocks.

In the tattered spray, I saw the face.

"There you are!" Wind hissed.

THE SHADOW
OF THE WIND
Mile 97, 4:39 a.m.

Wind's voice was as welcome as a dentist's drill.

"I suppose you've come for your shadow," I said.

"Did you find it?" Wind hissed.

Its voice sounded like sand blowing across a parking lot. I reminded myself that none of this was real. Hallucinations can't hurt you, Dad had assured me. They're just a reminder to eat more sugar.

"I have good news," I said.

"You do?"

"Yes. But first, I have a question."

Wind swirled between the trees. A thick branch snapped and crashed to the rocks below.

"Why do you steal things?" I asked.

A monster wave clobbered the shore. "I never steal," Wind said. "I just move stuff around."

"That's not true," I said. "You stole my dad's pants. There's no way you could have got them unless — "

A cloud of sand swirled in the air. The lightning storm was coming closer.

"I don't know what you're talking about," Wind said.

I leaned over and coughed. It was getting hard to breathe. Each time I exhaled, I wondered if I'd have the strength to pull another breath of air back into my lungs.

"And what were you doing with *my* song?" I said, raising my voice. "There's no way you could have got that paper unless — "

"Are you going to give me my shadow, or what?"

"Stupid Wind," I said. "You never had a shadow."

"What?"

"There's nothing to you!" I shouted. "You're nothing but thin air!"

The howling wind dropped away to nothing.

"That's right!" I shouted. "You're completely invisible! You don't have a shadow because you can't block the light!"

Far away, thunder hammered the mountains. It rumbled over the valley and then slowly echoed into silence.

"But everything has a shadow," Wind whispered.

"Not everything," I said.

Lightning flashed again, revealing mountains of charcoal cloud. A blast of air threw me against a tree.

"Name one other thing that doesn't have a shadow!" Wind shrieked.

"That's easy," I spluttered. "Memories."

Another wave hit the shore, and spray lashed my face. "Don't be mad," I cried. "It's okay not to have a shadow. There are other types of shadows that you can — "

"Shut *up*!" said Wind. "Shut up *now*!"

Something stung my skin. My eyes were full of grit. Wind was running around on the beach, spraying sand in all directions.

Then, very quickly, everything went dark, as if someone had drawn a curtain across the moon. I could hear the tree-tops hissing like snakes. A bitter smell filled the air. There was a deafening *crack* and then a blinding flash.

Through a thick crust of sand, I could make out the shadows of writhing trees. Then everything went dark again.

I staggered down to the shore to flush out my eyes. The lake churned and the waves rushed at me like rabid dogs. One crash of thunder followed another, and between the crashes I could hear the sound of someone screaming.

"Kara!" I shouted. "Kara, is that you?"

No answer. My eyes were blurry and wet. The thunder was deafening, but I could still hear someone wailing.

"Dad?" I shouted. "Dad, are you there?"

The screaming sounded more like a man than a woman, and I worried that it was Kern, the bandit. I crouched down beside a boulder. My eyeballs felt like they'd been scrubbed with steel wool.

Suddenly, an ice pick stabbed my neck. Something else took a bite out of my arm.

Hail!

I blinked away the rest of the sand, ran to the edge of the forest and crouched down.

For the next 3 minutes, hailstones crashed down. It felt like I was in a blizzard of molars. In no time, the forest was carpeted in grey slush. The air filled up with the tang of pine, as if someone had run a lawnmower through the treetops.

Then, as suddenly as it had started, the hail stopped. A hush fell over the forest. The air was still and fragrant.

A high-pitched whistle filled my ears. It was far away, but rushing closer every moment.

"What the . . . ?"

It was Wind. It sped across the lake with a papery sound, like handfuls of dry rice being thrown on a kitchen floor. Lightning flashed every 2 or 3 seconds, and through the choppy light I could see a wall of rain. It swept across the lake like a huge grey blanket. Then, like a bulldozer, it smashed into the forest.

The trees thrashed, yanking at their roots. Rocks flew through the air like ice cubes in a blender.

"There's no point breaking stuff!" I shouted. "It won't make your shadow appear."

"Maybe not," roared Wind. "But it makes me feel better!"

There was a splintering *crack*, and a giant spruce tree collapsed. I realized that I needed to get out of the forest, so I ran back down to the edge of the lake. Colossal waves battered the shore, and sheets of spray lashed the rocks.

Then a new sound arose — a throttling hum. It sounded like an airplane taking off.

In the dim light I saw a rope fall out of the clouds. The hum turned into a scream. The rope was a tornado.

THE SHRINE
Mile 97, 4:51 a.m.

Trees flew through the air like laundry from a clothes line. Other stuff too — rocks, branches, an old rowboat. A flurry of pink flags whipped past my eyes. The trail markers! I thought. The path home. Gone!

The weirdest part was the air. It was impossible to breathe. It was clogged with dirt and water. It was like inhaling mud.

Lightning flashed and rain sheeted. It felt like a fire hose was being shot at my head. I kept worrying about the other runners. Kara, Kern, even the Dirt Eater.

I wedged myself down between two boulders. There was a series of pops, and another tree crashed down. The roar of the tornado got louder and louder. Then something hit my head, and everything went black.

* * *

Later, I woke to the smell of damp cedar. A cluster of stars shone down between the treetops. The lake was still, and the trees had stopped swaying. In the dripping silence, I could hear the croaking of frogs.

I pulled myself out of my hidey-hole. My head hurt, my arms hurt, my shoulders hurt too. My gums hurt, swallowing hurt, breathing hurt — everything hurt. I brushed the hair off my forehead. Even my hair hurt!

I tugged off my shoes and held them upside down. Rivers of brown sludge poured out onto the ground. The duct tape was still holding my feet together, but two of my toenails had turned completely black.

Toenails are supposed to be pink, not black.

I felt sick — like something in my stomach had curdled.

I peeled off my tights and T-shirts and wrung them out. My chest was covered with purple welts. I put my wet shirts back on and tried to stand up, but a spike of pain shot up my spine. I slumped back down against a pile of rocks.

Bad thoughts swam through me like eels. My gels were gone. My cookie bag was gone too. And I had no idea where the trail was anymore.

Just then, as I was trying to decide what to do, a stone popped loose from the pile of rocks at my back. I twisted sideways and shone my light into the hole.

Something glinted. I reached inside.

SYDNEY WATSON WALTERS: Don't tell me. The Shrine.

QUINN: Yeah, but it wasn't much to look at. I'd expected a fountain, or a stone building or something. This was just a shabby pile of rocks.

SYDNEY WATSON WALTERS: And you expected something more than that?

QUINN: I'm getting to that.

I reached inside the cairn and felt around. My fingers touched a metal box. I pulled it out. It was heavy — maybe a couple of kilos. Three lines had been stamped on the lid:

> *For runners left behind,*
> *And for those who give us courage.*
> *We give thanks at this shrine.*

I unlatched the clasp on the lid of the box and opened it up. It was filled with a bunch of junk. Silver dollars, dried flowers, shoelaces braided into crosses.

What a disappointment.

I unzipped my fanny pack and pulled out my photo, glad that Mom had had it laminated.

I slid the photo into the box, flipped down the lid and slid it back inside the cairn.

SYDNEY WATSON WALTERS: Tell me about the picture.

QUINN: The one of my family? It was nothing special. Just a picture of the four of us, all together. Dad was wearing his uniform and he had his hand on my shoulder. Mom and I were wearing our Sunday clothes. Ollie was holding his gecko, Boo.

SYDNEY WATSON WALTERS: What did it feel like, leaving that picture at the Shrine?

QUINN: It didn't feel like anything, really. I'd promised Dad I'd leave something there for him, so I guess I was glad that I could keep my promise.

SYDNEY WATSON WALTERS: Didn't you feel anything else?

QUINN: What do you want me to say, that I cried? I didn't. I'd had it with crying. Mom's shrink says that crying will make me feel better, but I'd done it a bunch of times, and it didn't change anything. That doctor didn't know what he was talking about. You can cry all you want, but the world is still a total suckfest when you're done.

After I plugged up the hole in the Shrine, I dug around in my fanny pack. Kneecap's phone was soaking wet and out of juice. For a second I thought I'd wrecked it, but when I clicked the spare battery into place, the screen lit up.

At last, I thought! A little good luck!

I dialed the Albatross, but nothing happened. I stared at the screen. NO SERVICE, it said.

I climbed to the top of the pile of rocks, thinking I might get better reception. I called Kneecap's house. NO SERVICE, the phone said.

Then I went a bit crazy. I couldn't believe all my bad luck. I picked up a rock from the top of the Shrine and whipped it at the forest as hard as I could. It glanced off a pine tree with an ear-splitting crack.

"It's about time you cleaned yourself up!" I shouted. Then I reached down and picked up another rock.

This time the rock smashed against a boulder. "How's *that* for a surprise?" I yelled.

I jumped down off the cairn and pulled a bunch of rocks loose. "Take *that*!" I screamed. "And *that*! And *THAT*!"

I threw the rocks as hard as I could. My heart was hammering and my vision was a blur. Finally, when I ran out of loose rocks, I reached back into the cairn and pulled out the tin box. I guess I would have thrown that too, but then Kneecap's phone began to ring.

For a moment I didn't know what to do. I sat down with the box and stared at the phone. The screen said two words: CALLING: SCHEURMANN.

Part of me wanted to chuck the phone into the forest. I'm not sure what stopped me from doing that.

"Hello?" I said finally.

"Quinn?" said Mom.

"Hi," I said.

My throat thickened up and I felt a sobbing in my chest. Be cool, I told myself. Breathe deep.

"Thank God!" Mom said. "I've been calling for two hours!"

"Really?" I said. "I guess the network was down."

"Are you okay? There's a tornado warning."

"I know," I said. "The storm just ended."

"Really? It's pouring here!"

"Don't worry," I said. "I'm fine."

No I'm not! I wanted to scream. No I'm not!

I felt like I'd been run over by a train.

"Have you crossed the finish line yet?" Mom asked.

"Not exactly," I said.

My fingernails were blue and my whole body was shivering. I was actually having trouble hanging on to the phone.

"Where are you?" Mom asked.

"At the Shrine."

The phone line crackled between us.

"You must be soaking," she said. "Are you warm enough?"

"Toasty warm," I said. I clenched my jaw so my teeth wouldn't chatter.

"We'll be at the base camp in an hour," Mom said. "Hang on; I'll wake up your brother."

I listened to the rainstorm pounding my house, far away.

"Hello?" said Ollie.

"Hey bro, how's it going?"

"Quinn?" Sleep in his voice. "What time is it?"

"Nearly five," I said.

Thunder sounded over the phone.

"Is it storming where you are?" Ollie asked.

"Not anymore," I said. "It was bad for a while. My fault. I gave some bad news to Wind."

Ollie said nothing to this. I rubbed my feet. One of my toenails came off in my fingers.

"I need your help, Ollie," I said. "I don't think I can finish this race."

"Do you still have two feet?" Ollie asked.

I looked down at the ground. My feet, wrapped in decaying duct tape, looked like used-up teabags.

"Sort of," I said.

"Can you move them?" said Ollie.

I wiggled my feet back and forth. Two toes had turned purple, but the rest seemed okay. "Yes," I said.

"Then you're going to finish the race," said Ollie.

I appreciated what he was doing, trying to boost my spirits like that. But wait. That's a lie. I didn't appreciate that at all! I actually wanted to yell: Listen, you pig stick, you've been sleeping in a warm bed all night long, so why don't you just —

"How many miles do you have left?" Ollie asked.

"Three," I said. "But I think I broke some toes, and the tornado blew all the course flags away."

164

DNF, I thought. Those letters didn't sound so bad. Actually, they sounded a bit like a prayer.

"Want to hear a knock-knock joke?" Ollie asked.

"Come on, Ollie," I pleaded. "I've lost my way. My body is toast. And I'm freezing to death!"

"Knock knock," said Ollie.

"OLLIE!" I shouted.

"Knock knock."

I sighed. "Who's there?"

"Accordion," said Ollie.

"Accordion who?"

"Accordion to the TV, the wind is gonna blow all day!"

Ollie roared with laughter at the other end of the line.

I didn't laugh. Jokes were the last thing I needed just then.

"The storm blew the trail markers away," I repeated. "Even if I had the strength, I wouldn't know which way to run!"

"Sure you do," Ollie said. "You've got GPS."

He was right. I'd seen the app on Kneecap's phone. All I needed were the Base Camp's coordinates.

"You can do it," he said. "I know you can."

You skid mark, I thought, I feel like crap. I'd rather be dead than have to run any farther.

Ollie was quiet on the other end of the phone. Kneecap was right, I suddenly realized. I *am* a fun vampire.

"Ollie?" I said.

"What?" he said.

"I can't do it. I'm quitting."

I hadn't known I was going to say that. But now that I

had, relief flooded through my body. I'd run 97 miles. I'd crossed paths with a bear, I'd nearly fallen off a train bridge, and I'd nearly been swallowed by a tornado.

"Why are you quitting?" Ollie asked.

"Because I'm hurt," I said.

"As much as we hurt when Daddy died?"

OLLIE'S WISE WORDS

Mile 97, 5:06 a.m.

SYDNEY WATSON WALTERS: Your father served in Afghanistan, isn't that right?

QUINN: Yeah. He was on his third tour of duty.

SYDNEY WATSON WALTERS: Do you remember the day that he left?

QUINN: Sort of. I thought his bus was coming at eight, not at six. Mom kept yelling at me to get up, get up.

Ollie came into my room. "Hurry up!" he pleaded. "He's leaving soon!" He sounded kind of choked up.

"Get lost," I said.

A few minutes later Dad came and sat on the edge of my bed. We'd fought the night before, so I pretended to be asleep. I heard the clomp of his boots and the rustle of his pants. "Gotta go, kiddo," he said and he leaned down and kissed my head.

Then he went. Climbed onto the bus and was gone.

SYDNEY WATSON WALTERS: What had you been fighting about the night before?

QUINN: Afghanistan. He'd already gone there twice. I didn't get why he had to go back.

"If you were a real father," I'd told him, "you'd stay with us."

SYDNEY WATSON WALTERS: What did he say to that?

QUINN: He kept talking about all the kids over there. How they had no food, no water, no education.

"How about *dads*?" I asked him. "Do they have any of those?"

"A lot of them don't," he said.

I said, "I know how they feel."

Dad counted to five beneath his breath.

"I watch the news, you know," I told him. "A lot of people think we shouldn't even be in Afghanistan."

"A lot of people are wrong," he said.

"Maybe you're the one who's wrong," I said.

SYDNEY WATSON WALTERS: It's been a terrible war. No one can argue with that. And it's the families of the soldiers who have sacrificed the most.

(Audience applauds)

QUINN: Okay, fine. But do you know how many times Afghanistan has been invaded? Dozens of times. Russia, Britain, Genghis Khan, the United States, they all invaded Afghanistan at one time or another.

Now — do you know how many of those invaders won? None of them. Not a single one. That's because Afghanistan is unwinnable. It doesn't take a lot of brains to figure that out.

(Long silence; audience fidgets)

168

I'm sorry. I shouldn't have said that. Do you need to go to a commercial now?

SYDNEY WATSON WALTERS: No, this is important. Your story is important.

QUINN: It's just that, in Afghanistan, everyone loses. Especially my family. We lost a lot.

SYDNEY WATSON WALTERS: Your dad was driving over a bridge outside of Kandahar . . .

QUINN: It was an IED — you know, Improvised Explosive Device. The whole right side of the carrier was blown in. Both of his legs were torn off.

(Long silence)

SYDNEY WATSON WALTERS: Take as much time as you need. Would you like a glass of water?

QUINN: Don't you get it, he lost his *LEGS*! The legs he used to go running with!

(Long silence)

SYDNEY WATSON WALTERS: It's okay, Quinn. It's not your fault. It's most definitely not your fault.

QUINN: But it is, don't you see? I pretended to be asleep. I never said goodbye. I never told him —

SYDNEY WATSON WALTERS: What? What didn't you tell your father?

QUINN: I never told him . . . that I love him.

Ollie was still quiet. Fingernails of light glimmered behind the hills.

"He's only been gone since November," Ollie said finally. "But I'm already starting to forget what he was like."

"That's not true," I said. "You remember his jokes. You've been telling them to me all through this race."

Ollie clicked his tongue like a tree frog.

"You also remember his stories," I said. "That one you told me last night, about Dad running the New York Marathon."

I rubbed my feet. The duct tape was peeling at the edges. Somewhere above me, an airplane rumbled through the sky.

"I remember something else about him," said Ollie.

"What's that?"

"Sometimes at night, when Mom had her book club over, Dad came into my room and played his ukulele."

"What songs did he play?" I asked.

"Songs he made up himself. He had this one about a whale who wishes he could fly."

"Do you remember how it went?" I said.

"I think so." And he sang:

> *Say hello!*
> *Wave goodbye!*
> *Swim today!*
> *Tomorrow we'll fly!*

I leaned back against the pile of rocks and listened to the water dripping from the trees. A burst of static hissed down the line, and I could hear Mom telling Ollie to hurry up and get dressed.

"How's Mom?" I said.

"Not so great," Ollie said. "I don't think she slept very much last night."

I could hear Ollie pulling open his dresser. Suddenly he said, "You should be nicer to her, you know."

"You think?" I said.

"Yeah. She misses Daddy too."

Snot was leaking out of my nose. I wiped it off on the back of my sleeve. I thought of Ollie, sitting in his bed, and the liquid light of his aquarium, and the sound of electric bubbles. Down the hall, in the fridge, cherry yogurt and cheese sticks. It all seemed a million miles away.

"I'm not really cheering you up, am I?" said Ollie.

"In some ways you are," I said. "But my feet are toast. I can't finish this race."

"You only have three more miles," said Ollie.

"In this mud," I said, "that's two hours of running."

"You've still got an hour before the cut-off," said Ollie.

"I don't care about the cut-off," I said.

"I know," Ollie said sadly. And then he said, "I always knew you wouldn't finish."

"What?" I said.

"I always knew you wouldn't finish."

There are only six words in the entire English language that are guaranteed to get an exhausted runner up and moving again. And Ollie had just said those six little words.

"Everyone else knows it too," Ollie said. "Grandma Sue, Auntie Lauren. Even Mom thinks you'll quit."

"You're wrong," I said.

"Want the GPS coordinates?" Ollie asked.

"Yes, go ahead."

THE KICKING OF SHINS

Mile 97, 5:29 a.m.

The GPS claimed I had 3 miles to go. But that was total crap.

Those 3 miles felt more like 30. They went on forever. They refused to end.

A purple glow blotted out the stars. Orange light nibbled at the edge of the horizon. It was 5:30 in the morning. I'd been running for 23½ hours.

Only 30 minutes left until the cut-off.

I shook myself awake and punched my quads to loosen them up.

"Let's go, dammit!" I said. *"Move!"*

Reluctantly, my legs obeyed.

Downed trees were everywhere, and the trail was scarred with oozing sinkholes and craters of brown water. From time to time I saw the glimmer of Hither Lake through the trees to my left. That was good. If the lake was on my left, I must be travelling south. The GPS confirmed that I was going the right way.

Still, it was slow going. The hills were greased with a shiny coat of mud. When I came to a deep ravine, I tried to get to the bottom without falling. What a joke! I wound up slaloming down the slope on two feet and then I did a face-plant into an oil slick of muck.

Too bad Kneecap isn't here to see this, I thought as I stood up and scooped the mud out of my ears.

Red-winged blackbirds began to sing. I took a step forward and sank into the earth. In a heartbeat, I'd sunk right up to my butt. I twisted my body sideways, yanking back my legs. When my feet popped into the air, both of my shoes were missing.

"Hey!" I shouted. "Give me back my shoes!"

I lay forward on my belly and reached my arm down into the oozing muck-hole. I had to get my shoulder right in there and press my cheek deep into the mud before I snagged the shoelaces with the tips of my fingers. When I finally got the shoes out, they were as black as tar. They looked like two enormous cow patties.

Eventually I got the shoes back on to my duct-taped feet. I ran on, slipping and sliding in the mud. Mosquitoes hummed all around me.

And then something strange happened. As I ran, I heard another runner behind me. I could hear him splashing through puddles and snapping tree branches. I stopped and turned around and waited for him to catch up. I waited for 2 minutes, maybe longer. But the mystery runner never appeared.

Uh-oh, I thought. I'm hearing things again.

I kept going. When I came to a swollen creek, I washed the mud off my face and arms. I heard the noises behind me again, and this time I could clearly see a light in the forest.

Thank God! I thought. I'm not going crazy after all!

I stopped and waited for another couple of minutes, but again, the mystery runner failed to appear. The light in the forest vanished between the trees as I watched. What the heck? I thought to myself.

In the end, I decided that it was probably my dad. He was watching out for me. He wanted to make sure that I was safe.

"Don't worry, Dad!" I yelled. "I've only got two more miles to go! And I'm still not dead! Hooray for not being dead!"

At the top of the next hill I took a break. The pale outline of Hither Lake was visible in the valley, and the ribbon of orange was thickening on the horizon. Ahead of me, a spear of light stabbed into the sky. What the heck is that? I wondered.

I ran toward the light and then I saw the lump.

A fallen runner was slumped against a tree. He was lying on his back. He was moaning in pain.

Aha! I thought. The Dirt Eater! I'd caught him!

But then I heard the voice. It wasn't a man.

"Where did I put my hair dryer?" she groaned.

Kara looked like a melted candle. Her eyes were scribbles. Her cheekbones had caved in.

I ran over to her. She looked like absolute crap.

"Quinn," she croaked. "Lucky Number Thirteen. Did you see my hair dryer? I lost it on the trail."

Her voice sounded crusty. She'd torn the flesh over one eye. Worse, she was shivering and her forehead felt hot.

"Are you okay?" I said, crouching down.

Kara closed her eyes. "Awesome possum," she muttered.

Her lips were white and glowed in the dark, as if she were wearing chalk-coloured lipstick. I hugged her until the worst of her shivering had passed, and then I dug an extra T-shirt out of my pack.

"Put this on," I said. "It's damp, but it's better than nothing."

I helped to pull it over her head. Her fingers weren't moving very quickly.

"Come on," I said. "We're almost at the finish." I tried pulling her to her feet.

Kara went into a coughing fit. "No thank you!" she choked. "I'm just taking a little nap."

"No you're not," I said and I tried to stand her up. I pulled her halfway to her feet, but her knees crumpled like a paper cup. She fell sideways, smacking my chin with her arm. Stung, I fell back against a cedar bush, and the water from the branches sprinkled down on me like rain.

"Let me go!" she cried. And then she started to laugh. She squeezed a handful of mud between her fingers and giggled as it oozed down her arm.

For a moment, I wasn't sure what to do. I looked at my GPS. We only had 1 mile to go.

One mile. 1600 metres. 5280 feet. That was all.

The fastest humans can run a mile in less than 4 minutes. We'd be lucky if we did it in 20.

Twenty minutes, I thought. Kara could go hypothermic in that time. I *needed* to get her to the finish line.

"Stand up!" I yelled. "Or I'll call 911! They'll drag you out of here on a stretcher!"

Kara stopped laughing. Her eyes went wide. "You wouldn't," she said.

"I absolutely would," I said. "And you'd get a DNF. Just think how embarrassing *that* would be."

She blinked twice, and this time her eyes seemed to focus.

"They have hair dryers at the finish line," I added.

Kara thought about this for precisely one second and then she abruptly held out her hand. I took it and somehow managed to pull her to her feet.

"I don't think I can do this," she muttered.

"Yes you can," I said. "You absolutely can."

The final mile of the Shin-Kicker is a long, downhill straightaway that runs along a narrow dirt road. We staggered along it, arm in arm. It took all of my strength just to keep Kara upright.

"What happened to your shoes?" I asked.

Kara looked down. Her feet were bare. "I guess I lost them in the mud," she said.

We weren't really running. We were barely even walking. If you'd seen us, you'd have thought we were escapees from an asylum.

Suddenly Kara stopped.

"What's wrong?" I asked.

"Don't you hear it?" she said.

Now that she mentioned it, I did. It was the sound of wet running shoes slapping on mud. Someone was running on the road behind us! So I hadn't been going crazy, after all!

Slap! Slap! Slap!

The sound was far away — but getting closer every second.

I turned to look, but it was too dark to see anything. Whoever it was, he wasn't wearing a headlamp. But we could sure hear those shoes.

"He's trying to sneak up on us," Kara said. "That's why he's got his headlamp turned off."

Slap! Slap! Slap!

The sound was getting louder. The runner couldn't be more than a couple hundred metres back.

"Come on!" said Kara. "Let's do this thing!"

Do what thing? I thought.

And then I realized. She wanted to RUN.

She started sprinting and pulled me behind her. "Yow! Yow! Yowch!" I cried.

It felt like my legs were being pressed through a cheese grater. And yet, somehow, we continued to stagger forward.

"What's the time?" Kara asked.

I looked at my watch. "Five fifty-five," I said.

She scowled. "And how far to the finish?"

I checked the phone's GPS. "Half a mile," I said.

"We still have a shot at those buckles!" Kara said.

We kept moving. But for every metre we travelled, whoever was behind us must have travelled two. His footsteps grew louder, and when I looked back, I could see splashes of dull light close to the ground.

But it was a strange thing. It wasn't light from a flashlight. It was something else. Something green.

Then, suddenly, I knew. I knew who it was. He could turn off his headlamp, but he couldn't turn off his socks. "It's the Dirt Eater!" I said.

"No!" said Kara. "How'd he get behind us?"

I pointed out the sock light. Kara groaned. "The storm must have thrown him off course," she said.

"Come on," I said. "We can't let him beat us."

Kara nodded, but our little sprint had sapped all her energy. She was slowing down again. At least her lips weren't white anymore.

Suddenly, I heard clapping.

"You guys look great!" someone barked. "You've run ninety-nine and three-quarter miles and you've still got a spring in your step!"

It was Bruce — wearing a yellow raincoat and rubber boots. The little kid at his side looked strangely familiar.

"How much farther?" Kara gasped.

"Only four hundred metres!" Bruce shouted.

"But someone's right behind you!" said the boy. "Pick it up! You're in first place!"

First place? Kara and I glanced at each other.

"It's true," Bruce said. "This race is yours to lose. Keep those legs moving! You're almost there!"

The little kid, I noticed, was wearing Star Wars jammies. He was holding a bowl of breakfast cereal. I suddenly realized who he was.

"Hey, Ollie," I said.

"Go, Quinn, GO!" he shouted.

Down the road I could see a long white banner. The banner had one word on it. The most beautiful word in the world:

FINISH

I could see people streaming out of the gatehouse. "Go for it, Ultra Boy!" a familiar voice shouted. That could only be Kneecap, I knew.

For the last time, I checked the GPS. It said: Miles Remaining: 0.1.

"How much farther?" Kara asked.

"About sixty seconds," I said.

And that was when the Dirt Eater passed us.

I'd heard his footsteps getting closer, but now he slipped past us like the easiest of ground balls. All I could do was watch him go. I knew I didn't have the strength to chase him.

"Nice pace, Monkey Boy," he sneered as he flew past.

"What was that?" Kara said. "What did you say?"

The Dirt Eater didn't answer; he just kept on running. His running shoes weren't even very muddy, I noticed.

"What did he say?" Kara asked.

"He was talking to me," I said. "He said, 'Nice pace, Monkey Boy.'"

Kara suddenly stopped running and sat down on the wet grass. Her hair and face were mapped with sweat.

"What are you doing?" I said. "You're almost there!"

She glared after the Dirt Eater, who was vanishing down the road. Her face was bright red. "You have to crush him," she said.

"No," I said. "You and I are finishing this together."

"No," she said. "There's no way I'll catch him. But you've got to beat that no-good cheater!"

I stared at her and then back at the Dirt Eater, who was charging up the road in front of us.

"GO!" shouted Kara. "Do it for me! Better yet, do it for your dad!"

Her eyes were rust-coloured and determined and tears were streaming down her face.

"You know about my dad?" I said.

"Of course," said Kara. "The guy is a legend."

And then, somehow, I broke into a run. It wasn't pretty; in fact, it was downright ugly, since my legs felt like they'd been dipped in cement.

The crowd cheered. "You can do it!" someone shouted.

I thought: Next person who tells me I can do it gets this cellphone straight in the head.

Suddenly I noticed someone running beside me. It was Ollie. He was running faster than me.

"Use your superpowers!" he shouted.

"What?" I said.

"Your superpowers!" Ollie screamed. "Your heart! Use your heart!"

Right — my big heart! I'd forgotten about that!

Then I saw Kneecap. "C'mon, Quinn!" she hollered. "KICK SOME SHINS!"

When I saw her there, something snapped. Electricity sizzled through my body and my legs felt full of juice. I leaned forward and remembered what my dad had said: "Your heart is stronger than you think."

I shot down the road, my legs spinning like pinwheels. The world blurred past me — trees, puddles, mud.

I could hear myself laughing and I heard the blood in my veins, and the volunteers were screaming, "Go! Go! Go!"

A strange feeling came over me then. For one moment, all my pain and anger were gone. Nothing hurt. Everything was peaceful. I couldn't even hear any voices in my head. For a moment, it felt like my heart had stopped beating. I even had this strange feeling that I'd become invisible.

Twenty metres from the finish, I sprinted past my mom, who was standing at the side of the road, clapping. Her cheeks were shiny and wet. Not far ahead, the Dirt Eater was slowing down — he thought he'd won the race already.

The finish line was 10 metres away. Then 5, then only 3. I flew past the Dirt Eater like he was standing still!

Me — Quinn Scheurmann. I won the Shin-Kicker 100.

I raised my arms as I crossed the line.

Time: 23 hours, 59 minutes, 32 seconds.

SYDNEY WATSON WALTERS: And Kneecap was filming the whole thing?

QUINN: Yeah. She uploaded the video later that afternoon. It went viral two days later, after Michelle Obama posted it on her blog. Six million people viewed it in three days.

SYDNEY WATSON WALTERS: And then you started getting invited to appear on TV shows like mine.

QUINN: Yeah. Life got a bit more colourful then.

THE LONG SHADOW
Mile 100

The volunteers clapped for 10 or 15 seconds, and someone stuffed a bottle of water into my hands. Behind me, I could hear the Dirt Eater cursing. People clapped for him too, though not as much.

Mom wrapped her arms around me and wouldn't let me go. She didn't seem to care that I was covered in mud.

"What are you doing winning?" she said. "You promised me you'd take it easy."

"I tried to!" I said. "But the tornado messed everything up!"

The Dirt Eater threw his water bottle at the ground so hard it bounced. I thought he was going to say something mean, but instead he just stomped off toward the toilets.

A few seconds later, Kara staggered across the line. People whooped and hollered as she knelt down in the road. I thought that she was going to throw up, but instead she bent her head to the ground and kissed the dirt.

"What time is it?" she said, looking up.

We all looked at the clock. It said 23:59:59.

"Yesss!" said Kara.

Somewhere in the valley, a chainsaw roared to life. I leaned over and started to cough.

"Hands above your head," said Mom. "Breathe deep."

I raised my arms and coughed some more. When the coughing fit ended, I leaned over and stretched out my back.

"What do you need?" Mom said. "Something to eat? Warm clothes?" Her eyes looked bruised, as if she hadn't slept.

"I could use some dry shoes and socks," I said.

Mom looked at my feet. My shoes were caked with mud, and the toes were bright red from the blood that had seeped through.

Mom took a deep breath. "I'll get the first-aid kit," she said. "Give me two minutes. I'll be back."

She dashed off. Kneecap and Ollie rushed over. "Way to go!" Ollie said. "That was EPIC!"

The camera was still rolling. "What happened to your head?" Kneecap asked.

"That's nothing," I said. "Wait till you see my feet."

Behind me, two volunteers helped Kara to the medical tent. She could barely walk, even with their support.

Ollie high-fived me. "I knew you could do it," he said. "You know that I was only kidding before, right?"

"I know," I said. "You did exactly the right thing."

He was still holding that bowl of cereal. That's when it hit me — it really was six in the morning. I really had been running for 24 hours. Not only that, I'd somehow won the race.

As if to confirm this, Bruce exploded out of the gate-house. He splashed through a puddle and held out his hand. "Congratulations!" he said. "Incredible effort."

"Thanks," I said.

He fished into his pocket and pulled out a silver belt buckle. A black bear leered at me from the centre of the medallion.

"Don't lose that," said Bruce. "Those things aren't easy to come by. I'm only handing out two of them this year."

"Don't you mean three?" I said. "Kara finished one second before the cut-off."

"Oh, she'll get one for sure," Bruce said. "But I'm not so sure about Ted Parker. There are some irregularities with his times."

Kneecap's face lit up. "Good!" she squealed. "That guy's a total cheater." She ran her finger over the engraving of the bear. "Kara was right," she said. "That thing is gorge-E-ous!"

"Hey, that reminds me," I said, "I need to give you this." I handed over her phone.

"Does it still work after all that rain?"

"It works perfect," I said. "It actually saved my life."

She handed back my belt buckle. It weighed a quarter kilo, easy. I pulled a muddy shoelace out of one of my train-ers, slung it through the clasps and tied the loop around my neck. At that moment, as far as I was concerned, that buckle was the most valuable piece of metal in the world.

"Sorry about that tornado," Bruce said.

"No probs," I said. "I've lived through worse."

Kneecap pulled her headphones down over her ears and lay down on a log.

"Your dad would be proud of you," Bruce said.

"You knew him?" Ollie asked.

"Of course," said Bruce. "Your old man paced me in this race, one time. He never set any speed records, but he was a great pacer. An awesome storyteller too, but you already know that."

I rubbed a sleeve across my nose.

"I heard about what happened," Bruce went on. "It didn't surprise me that he was serving his country. He was always looking out for others, that guy. He was one of the good ones. He left an awfully long shadow."

The sun was up now, turning the treetops gold, and the wet grass glinted at the edge of the road. Somewhere in the trees, a crow was screeching. I ran my tongue across the roof of my mouth. I had terrible breath. Ultra bad breath.

"Want a mug of hot chocolate?" Bruce asked.

"Yes please!" said Kneecap, jolting upright.

Bruce grinned and walked off toward the gatehouse.

"I'll help!" said Ollie, running after him.

A pair of toads, grim and ancient-looking, hopped across the silvery grass. I watched their progress and then noticed Kneecap's fingers, which were tapping out a rhythm against the side of her leg.

I went over and poked her in the ribs. "Hey," I said.

Her eyes opened a crack. "Hey, yourself," she said.

"Thanks for coming out," I mumbled.

Kneecap yawned and took off her headphones. "What was that?" she said.

"I said, Thanks."

"What for?" she asked.

"For running with me yesterday," I said. "And thanks for . . . I don't know . . . for everything else." I looked up at the sky. A pair of red-tailed hawks was circling. "I know I haven't been much of a friend this year . . . " I stopped. A mitten was stuck in my throat.

"Go on," Kneecap said. "I'm listening."

"What I wanted to say is . . . I'm sorry about that joke I told. At the Hallowe'en dance last year. It was so stupid. I meant to apologize . . . "

Kneecap yawned. "Forget it," she said. "We all say stupid things. Besides, we were just kids back then. And you had other stuff on your mind."

I lifted the belt buckle from around my neck. "Here," I said. "This belongs to you."

Kneecap's eyes bulged. "I can't take that," she said.

"Sure you can," I said.

I placed the buckle over her head. She grinned, and I could feel my heart speeding up.

Kneecap turned the buckle over in her hand. "But it's your keepsake," she said. "To remind you of the race."

"I don't need a reminder," I said. "This is one day I'll never forget."

Bruce and Ollie came out of the gatehouse carrying two mugs of hot chocolate each. It was the creamiest, most delicious hot chocolate I'd ever tasted. "Thanks," I said, giving Ollie a hug.

He squirmed free. "I did a good job as your pacer, right?"

"You sure did," I said. "I wouldn't have finished without you."

"What about me?" a voice called out.

I turned around. Mom was coming up the path. She had a bundle of clean clothes tucked under her arm.

"Thanks for your amazing genes, Mom!" I said. I stood up to hug her but — "YOW!" I shouted.

"Oh, my poor baby," Mom said. "Time to stretch out your quadriceps. You just ran a hundred miles, remember?"

She handed the clothes to Ollie and took my hand. "Come on," she said. "Try a lunge."

She lunged forward with one leg and then lowered the other leg down to the ground. "Your father swore by this one," she said.

"No way can I do that," I said.

"If you can run a hundred miles, you can do a simple stretch," said Mom. "Come on, Kneecap, help us out."

Kneecap jumped up and took my other hand. The three of us did a few lunges together.

"Hurts, doesn't it?" said Mom.

"A lot," I groaned.

"Good," said Mom. "Maybe that'll teach you to not run any more of these crazy races."

I sat back down in the chair. Mom smiled at me. Kneecap lay down on the log and put her headphones back on.

"I'm sorry I worried you," I said.

Mom shook her head. "It's okay," she said.

"No it's not," I said. "There was a *tornado*."

Mom dug around in the first-aid kit. The trees around us swayed in the wind and made a fizzing sound like root-beer foam rising up in a glass. Mom cleaned the cut on my forehead with a cotton ball and used her finger to rub ointment into the wound. She didn't talk.

"You should've *stopped* me," I told her. "Why didn't you stop me?"

She counted to ten under her breath. Then she began cleaning another cut — on my neck.

"I'm serious," I said. "You should have stopped me!"

I was shouting now, I couldn't help it. It felt like a whale was swimming up my throat.

"It's okay, Quinn," said Mom. "Remember to breathe."

"Why didn't you *stop* me?" I yelled. "You heard what Bruce said about the bears. You could have stopped me from running, but you didn't."

Mom peeled off my T-shirts, towelled my chest dry and then dropped a clean sweatshirt over my head. "You're a runner, Quinn," she said. "It's what you love to do. And nobody, not even me, should stop you from doing what you love."

My shoes came off. "Ow!" I shouted. "Take it easy!"

Mom looked at my feet and drew in her breath, but didn't say anything.

"But I could have been *hurt*," I went on, my heart pounding now. "I could have been hurt like *Dad*!"

The whale in my throat was thrashing its tail. Kneecap got up from the log where she was lying and walked away.

Mom took a pair of scissors from her purse. The duct tape was stuck to my feet pretty good.

"You should have stopped him from leaving," I cried. "All you had to do was tell him NO."

Mom sawed away at the tape with the scissors. "Your father was a soldier," she said. "He went because he needed to help others. That's who he was, that's why we loved him.

That's not something I had the power to stop."

The tape came off, bit by bit. Mom finished one foot and started on the other.

"I miss him," I mumbled into her hair.

"Me too," she said. "More than anything."

When she said that, I felt burning in my eyes and I knew that I was going to cry. When Dad died, I wasn't the only one who got hurt. Mom lost him too, but I hadn't really thought too much about that. I suddenly felt ashamed that I'd added to her pain. She'd been worried about this race, and I'd signed up for it anyway. I'd only been thinking about myself.

The whale was swimming out through my eyes, and suddenly I was crying like a baby. My body folded like a sheet of paper, and I cried silently, like a little kid, with my mouth wide open.

"I never said goodbye to him," I sobbed.

"That's all right," said Mom. "You're doing it now."

I cried so hard I could barely breathe. Mom wrapped her arms around me and kissed the top of my head.

"I hid one of my songs in his pocket," I said. "A nasty song, about how much I hated the war."

"We all hated the war," Mom said.

"I know," I said, "but we weren't supposed to say it."

I felt like I was falling from a terrible height. Like I was on top of the CN Tower and it was crumbling to the ground.

"We'll never be happy again," I snuffled.

"Yes we will," said Mom. "Some day we will."

My body clenched and rocked back and forth. This crying business was harder than running.

"You'll figure this out," Mom whispered in my ear. "But you can't keep locking yourself away in your room, Quinn. Ollie and I miss your father too. The three of us need to talk about him *together*."

She pulled some tissues out of her purse and wiped a bunch of crud off of my face. I cried until they were all used up. Mom found another packet, and I went through that one too.

But here's the funny thing. The more I cried, the better I was, until I felt as though I was floating up into the air. I looked at Mom and she was crying with me, and then suddenly, for no reason, we both started to laugh.

For a while, we laughed so hard we couldn't stop. Ollie came running over. "What's so funny?" he asked.

"I don't know," Mom gasped. She looked at me. "Do you?"

I shrugged.

Ollie looked confused. "Are you guys laughing or crying?" he asked. "You sound like you're laughing, but you look like you're crying."

Mom looked at me, and we broke into laughter again.

"Just tell me if you're happy or sad," Ollie said. "You should be able to answer that, at least."

Another runner was crossing the finish line. He was old and hunched over. It was the bandit — Kern!

Mom wiped the tears away from her eyes. She said, "We're happy, I think. Aren't we, Quinn?"

The sun was rising over the hills, and the trees were sparkling, as if ginger ale had been poured all over them. Ollie's question seemed impossible to answer — I was both happy *and* sad, which sounds weird, I know. The bandit's crazy laugh echoed through the valley. I looked at the finish line and saw him toss his wineskin in the air.

SYDNEY WATSON WALTERS: And then you came home?

QUINN: Not quite yet. First I inhaled two plates of spaghetti and meatballs and then we stuck around to watch the other runners finish. Most people crossed the finish line on their own steam, but a few people were brought out on horseback. We whooped and hollered for all of them.

SYDNEY WATSON WALTERS: What about Kara? What became of her?

QUINN: She spent an hour in the medical tent and then she came out and cheered along with everyone else. She'd showered and changed into dry sweats and a hoodie, and I barely recognized her, she looked so hot.

    She cheered with us for a couple of hours, eating bacon-and-egg sandwiches and drinking hot chocolate. Finally she had to go.

    "My kids will be waiting for me to fix some breakfast," she said. "But don't forget to Friend me. We could do some training runs together!"

SYDNEY WATSON WALTERS: And then?

QUINN: Have you ever tried squeezing into a hatchback after you've run a hundred miles? It's not fun.

My legs felt twitchy, as if electricity was running through them, and I kept crossing and uncrossing them to get them to calm down.

Mom drove us down the long gravel road back to the highway. "Don't Stop Believin'" was playing on the radio. Kneecap grinned at me in the mirror and sang along in the back seat. Ollie rested his head against the window and closed his eyes.

I sat in the front seat and watched the trees blur past my window. We drove farther in 15 minutes than I could've run in 3 hours.

I saw a sign for a railroad crossing.

"Better slow down here," I warned Mom.

"These tracks haven't been used in years," she said.

"Better safe than sorry," I said.

She slowed the car down. No trains were coming.

"Okay," I said. "Now let's make some time."

Author's Note

I've run a bunch of races like the one described in this book. After the first, my nieces and nephews asked me what I'd seen while jogging through the forest all night long.

"Nothing much," I said. "Just a whole bunch of trees."

The kids were disappointed by this answer. And so, after my next race, I made a point of telling better stories. I described the hidden valley wriggling with hoop snakes, the bears I'd seen playing shinny hockey, and the shrine where lost runners bury their secrets.

The farther I ran, the more the stories grew . . . until they eventually became the novel in your hands.

So, a huge shout-out to my nieces and nephews — who inspired this story, lent their names to some of the characters, helped me with the jokes and dialogue, and even shared early versions of the book with their classmates. You all deserve a finisher's medal:

Aaron, Alex, Ali, Ben, Benjamin, Brody, Caelan, Caitlin, Caleb, Christopher, Daniel, Darcie, Grace S., Grace W., Jackson, Julia, Julian, Kara, Kelsey, Kiernan, Leonardo, Lucy-Claire, Luke, Monty, Madelaine, Maggie, Mateos, Nate, Oliver, Olivia, Parisinia, Quinn, Ray, Riley, River, Rowan, Rylee, Sacha, Skyler, Sofia, Sydney, Tahnee, Tobias, Zoe.

About the Author

DAVID CARROLL has successfully competed in five 100-mile races, including the Haliburton Forest Trail Run and the Sulphur Springs 100. He's run the Boston Marathon twice, and many other marathons and half-marathons. His favourite running fuel is PB&J sandwiches.

Ultra is his first novel.